Total-E-Bound Publishing books by T.A. Chase:

The Four Horsemen
Pestilence
War
Famine
Death

I0570501

Anthologies:
Unconventional at Best: Ninja Cupcakes

Out of Light into Darkness

The Beasor Chronicles

GYPSIES

T.A. CHASE

Gypsies
ISBN # 978-1-78184-518-9
©Copyright T.A. Chase 2012
Cover Art by Posh Gosh ©Copyright July 2012
Interior text design by Claire Siemaszkiewicz
Total-E-Bound Publishing

Published in 2012 by Total-E-Bound Publishing, Think Tank, Ruston Way, Lincoln, LN6 7FL, United Kingdom.

Total-E-Bound Publishing is an imprint of Total-E-Ntwined Limited.

GYPSIES

Dedication

Thank you to all my readers who keep asking me when my next book is coming out. You're the reason why I keep writing, so I don't disappoint you. Thank you to my wonderful editor as well. Without you, the story wouldn't be nearly as good as it ends up.

Chapter One

On most nights, being an ordinary Beasor didn't bother Alden. He liked tending bar at his pub, and not having to worry about whether people liked him for who he was, or for what he could do for them. In Alden's world, there were four types of Beasor, and being an unremarkable one suited him.

Well, usually it did, but tonight something bothered him, and it had to do with his best friend, Percy. His friend was one of the extraordinary Beasors, and, as such, found himself constantly surrounded by hangers-on and leeches. They were all trying to get something from Percy. The way others fawned over and tried to use Percy upset Alden, but as long as it didn't bother Percy, Alden let it go.

Bright laughter lifted over the dull murmur of the crowd, and Alden glanced over to see Percy in the middle of a group. Percy caught his gaze and smiled at him. Alden grunted as desire kicked him in the gut, pooling in his groin. Thank the God he stood behind the bar, and no one could see the effect of Percy's attention on his body.

"Gypsies are a little like the angels those people on Earth talk about all the time, huh?"

Alden turned to see Chal, a regular customer at the pub, leaning on the bar with a knowing look on his face. He poured Chal his usual mug of dark ale and set it in front of his friend.

"Sometimes I think Gypsies know the effect they have on people, so they take advantage of it," Alden muttered as he flagged down one of his waitresses and put another glass of Pillian wine on her tray. "Take it to Percy. He should be empty by now."

"Yes, sir." She strolled through the customers with ease.

"Does he know you're in love with him?"

Alden ignored Chal's question, grabbing a towel to dry the clean glasses. The other bartenders had things under control, so he had time to chat with Chal.

"When did you get back?"

Chal took a swig from his mug, wiping his sleeve across his mouth when he was done. "Earlier today. It was a simple pick-up for one of my usual customers. Wasn't that big a deal."

"It's good to see you back." Alden leaned over and patted Chal on the arm. "Oh, by the way, I have an order of Pillian wine waiting for me on Clausen Three. Do you think you could make a run over there to get it for me?"

Being a Tramp, Chal could travel between the universes without harm, and Alden paid Chal to pick up deliveries of rare liquor and wines. Chal shoved his hand through his short brown hair and nodded.

"Let me check my schedule, but I think I can go in a day or two."

Alden shrugged. "There's no rush. Percy's the only one who drinks it, so I like to have some on hand for him."

Chal snorted and shook his head. "Seriously, man, why haven't you told him?"

"Told who?"

Both of them looked up to see Percy standing at the bar, his long blond hair glinting in the low light of the pub. His lavender eyes darted between Alden and Chal like he had a feeling they were sharing secrets without him. Stupid really, because Alden only ever kept one secret from Percy and he wasn't about to spill his guts about loving his best friend as more than a friend.

"Tell you, your groupies need to be more careful. They almost knocked one of my waitresses over in their rush to fawn over you." Alden winked, letting Percy know he was joking.

Percy flipped his hair over his shoulder, and perched his hand on his hip. "Well, dear, just point her out to me, and I'll give her a big tip."

"You know she'll want more than just your tip, Percy, no matter the size." Chal burst out laughing when Percy's mouth dropped open in shock.

Alden joined in the mirth, while Percy blushed. Alden reached across the bar to pat his friend on the shoulder.

"All my employees know you prefer male parts to female parts, Percy."

Percy huffed in annoyance, but didn't move away from them. "You both are so childish."

"Maybe, but you still love us." Alden grinned.

"You're right." Percy glanced over his shoulder as someone shouted his name. "Damn. I'm going to go hide upstairs for a while, Alden. If that one leaves, call me."

"Is he bothering you?"

Alden didn't like any of his customers being harassed, but he was extremely protective of Percy. A Gypsy's abilities to deal with animals or manipulate nature made them prime property, even though no one was supposed to own them. The High Council regulated everything the magical Beasors did, and how the regular Beasors treated them.

Sometimes it was difficult, as Gypsies were beautiful and very sexual. Everyone wanted them, and while for the most part, Gypsies weren't picky about whom they slept with, they did want it to be their choice. At least Percy preferred to chase his bed partners. Just because he'd never chosen Alden didn't make Alden bitter or anything.

Also, their abilities to talk to animals and work weather magic brought them to the attention of unscrupulous people who would kidnap them and steal their powers. Alden understood how rare it was to have a Gypsy as a friend, and a roommate as well. Normally, Gypsies stayed in secure compounds because they were so valuable.

"He won't take no for an answer, and I'm getting tired of repeating myself." Percy took a sip from the wine glass he held.

"Then go on up. I'll have the guys keep an eye on him. If he leaves, I'll call you."

"Thanks. You're a doll." Percy leaned over and kissed Alden's cheek.

Alden watched Percy dodge the clingy hands of people who wanted to bask in the reflected glow of the Gypsy. Chal snorted and, when Alden glanced at him, the Tramp shook his head.

"I've never seen anyone crush so hard as you. I don't know why you just don't tell him how you feel, Alden. Percy's not going to make fun of you or blow you off. If you're lucky, he'll blow you."

Alden tossed the towel in his hand at Chal. "As crude as you are, I can't believe you have any friends. I don't want to be another one of those people who wants something from Percy. We've been friends for so long, I'm afraid everything will change if I tell him."

Chal frowned. "I never understood that thought process. How do you know things will change if you tell him? Maybe he feels the same way about you, and is afraid to tell you."

"Percy isn't afraid of anything," Alden stated confidently.

"Just because he's gorgeous and powerful doesn't mean he's not insecure. None of us are so confident that there aren't things we're afraid of." Chal pushed his mug towards Alden with a quick tap of his finger to the rim. "I come across as obnoxious and arrogant, but I have issues just like any other man."

Alden took the hint, and poured Chal more ale.

"I'm not ugly or anything. I mean most of my lovers seemed to think I was attractive, but Percy could have any Beasor he wanted. Hell, he could have any person in any of the multiple universes if he wanted them. Why would he pick me?"

"If I have to explain, you're not ready to say a word to him." Chal drained his mug in one gulp. He banged it on the counter before pushing off. "I'm going to mingle and take some lucky person home for the night. I'll get a hold of you about the Pillian pick-up."

"Thanks, and good luck." Alden put the dirty glass in the sink behind him before flagging down one of his bouncers. "I need you to keep an eye on that guy right there."

He nodded towards the man Percy had pointed out. His head bouncer grunted in acknowledgement.

"If he leaves, let me know, but if he causes any problems for anyone here, toss him out on his ass."

"He bothering Percy?" Reagan gave him a knowing look.

Alden ground his teeth together while he grabbed control of his anger. Why was he getting upset with everyone tonight? It wasn't like he'd tried to hide how he felt about Percy. He just hoped his friend hadn't picked it up.

"Yes, but there are a few other Gypsies in here, so I don't want him annoying any of them."

"Yes, sir." Reagan moved over, a veritable avalanche of muscle and attitude.

Alden turned away, filling an order without worrying about Reagan or the other bouncers. They would take care of things. Alden's pub was a neutral place where Gypsies, Tramps, Thieves, and regular Beasors could mingle without having fights or arguments breaking out when the magical Beasors turned the others down.

Admittedly, when Alden first started to enforce the rule, it was to keep Percy happy and safe, but, once the rest of the magical Beasors heard about Alden's rule, they flocked to his pub, making it one of the most popular in the capital city of Catalai.

The phone behind the bar rang, and Alden knew who was calling before he even answered.

"He's not gone yet, Percy," he said, tucking the receiver between his head and his shoulder.

"Damn. I hate being forced to hide out," Percy whined.

Alden smiled, picturing Percy pouting in his mind. "I'm sorry. I can have Reagan and the guys throw him out, if you want."

Percy sighed. "No. I'm just not in a good mood. It's been a long week, and I was looking forward to relaxing with some friends."

Glancing around him, Alden noticed his employees had everything under control. The pub was busy, but not anything they couldn't handle. He made a decision.

"What do you want to eat? I'll order something from the deli across the street, and we'll have dinner together. I'll bring up another bottle of that Pillian wine you like."

"Oh, I can't let you do that, Alden. You need to work. I'm just being grumpy." Percy protested like Alden knew he would.

"I hired some pretty competent people who can run the bar without me. I'll be up as soon as the food is delivered." He hung up before Percy could say anything else.

He called the deli and placed an order for takeaway before informing Greta that he was leaving for the night. She knew to call him if they needed an extra pair of hands. It wasn't like he lived far away or anything.

His apartment was right above the bar, so it was easy to come and go whenever he wanted. Tonight, he wanted to spend time with Percy instead of mingling with customers. Alden took off his apron and tossed it over the edge of the bar. As he made his way through the crowd, he stopped to chat with friends and regular customers.

By the time Alden got outside, it was time to pick up his order. He raced across the street, grabbed the food and went back into the pub. Greta had a bottle of wine all ready for him to snatch up as he went past. Alden smiled his thanks at her, and she winked.

Leaving by a side door, Alden tried not to think about how much he enjoyed spending time with Percy, just the two of them. He was a homebody, plain and simple. He didn't need grand adventures to be happy, but Percy wasn't the same.

From the moment Percy had come into his full powers, he'd been travelling around the world, and through the universes. Alden doubted a universe existed that Percy hadn't been to, and that worldliness was one of the many things Alden loved about Percy. Alden understood that Percy needed adoration. He needed people flattering him.

As odd as it seemed, Percy's parents were disappointed in him. They hadn't wanted another Gypsy in the family, as even though his father had wanted to create a dynasty of Gypsies, they'd hoped Percy would be a Thief, because they wanted to garner even more wealth through his powers. More than they could with him being a Gypsy. Yet, from the instant Percy had opened his lavender eyes, his parents had done their level best to cut Percy down. Once Alden had realised how terrible Percy's family was, he'd vowed to be there for Percy without judging or criticising him. Alden wasn't perfect at it, but he tried, and that was what mattered.

He kicked the door, since he couldn't open it with his hands full. Percy opened it for him, and Alden swallowed his moan. How could he have forgotten that Percy would have changed his clothes? Alden was glad the length of his shirt covered his groin, because there wasn't any way he could stop his body from reacting.

Percy dressed in normal going-out clothes was a sight to behold, but when Percy decided to stay in he wore as little as possible. A short, dark purple cotton robe hung off Percy's slender shoulders, open to reveal his nicely toned chest and stomach. Alden didn't need to see Percy's ass to know it was tight and cute as hell. He closed his eyes, took a deep breath, and opened his eyes to smile at Percy.

"Dinner is served, my lord." Alden managed an off-balance bow, without spilling anything.

"You're being silly," Percy pointed out, taking the bottle of wine and holding the door, so Alden could walk in.

"But it made you smile, and now all is right in my world." He winked as he went past Percy, hoping Percy would think he was teasing.

Percy rolled his eyes, and smacked Alden on his arm. "You're such a joker. I'm starving, and you took your time bringing me food."

"I had to wait for the sandwiches to be made. Maybe if you learned how to cook, you wouldn't have to wait for me to bring you supper." Alden continued on to the kitchen where he set the food down. He turned to watch Percy wander in.

"I'm pretty and magical. How much more should people expect me to do? Aren't you here to take care of me?" Percy fluttered his eyelashes at Alden.

Alden bit his tongue and looked away. Damn, why did Percy have to be so gorgeous? But, then again, Alden had the feeling that if Percy were just as plain as he was Alden would still take care of him. There was something about Percy that cried out to Alden, and, no matter how much Alden tried to deny it, he couldn't ignore it.

"Here." He shoved one of the takeaway containers at Percy. "I'll get the drinks."

Percy frowned at him for a moment, before taking the food and wandering back out to the living room. Alden opened the Pillian wine, poured out a glass for Percy, and got a bottle of ale for himself. He returned to where Percy sat, and joined him on the couch, setting his wine on the table in front of him. Alden leant back and rested his bottle on his stomach.

"You aren't eating?" Percy had opened the container, and taken a bite.

Alden shook his head. "I'm not hungry, and I don't need to gain weight like some people I know."

He eyed Percy, and his friend bowed his head.

"Sorry. I try to gain it, but working my magic burns calories, and I can't ever seem to get bigger."

Shit! Alden hadn't meant to make Percy feel bad about himself. He reached over and covered Percy's hand with his. A spark of electricity rocketed through him, landing firmly in his groin.

"Honey, I wasn't complaining about you." He stopped and thought about it. "Okay, so I was complaining a little, but not because I think you aren't perfect the way you are. I just worry that you're getting too skinny, and it's not healthy for you."

Sighing, Percy scooted over until he leaned into Alden's body. Alden wrapped his arm around Percy's shoulders, holding his best friend close to him.

"I know you're taking care of me because you love me, Alden."

Panic shot through Alden. How had Percy figured that out? Alden had tried so hard not to be another one of Percy's admirers. He wanted to mean more to Percy than that.

"I mean, I'm your best friend, right? So, of course, you love me, and you want me to be healthy. I'll try to be better about eating and stuff like that."

The tension in Alden's body relaxed at Percy's words. He ran his hand over Percy's hair. "You're right, Percy. I want you healthy because you're my best friend in all the universes. I don't know what I'd do without you."

"Be terribly bored, and work way too much," Percy teased.

Alden didn't reply, but he agreed. Without Percy around to draw him away from his bar, Alden tended to bury himself in work. Aside from his customers, Alden wouldn't have many friends if Percy wasn't there to drag him out once in a while.

He watched as Percy ate every bite of food. When Percy had finished, Alden took the container and put it on the end table, and he settled back to hold Percy close to him. Percy didn't seem interested in talking, so Alden let the silence drift and grow, encasing them in quiet calm. One of the many things he loved about Percy was how they could go for hours without talking, and yet it didn't feel uncomfortable. Most of Percy's friends wouldn't believe Percy could be quiet for more than a minute.

* * * *

Percy breathed in the scents of sweat, ale, and male surrounding Alden, who hadn't had a chance to change his clothes when he'd got to their apartment. Percy had a reputation for being fastidious and, at times, a neat freak, but he didn't mind when Alden smelt like he'd been working all day. He wanted to bury his nose against the triangle of skin at the base of

Alden's throat and sniff, but he didn't think Alden would understand.

He lost track of how long they sat on the couch, wrapped in each other's arms. Did other best friends sit like that? Did other best friends rely on each other to the extent Percy relied on Alden?

Somehow Percy doubted it, and most people would think his reliance on Alden bordered on the unhealthy. Yet Percy knew Alden didn't care what other people thought, and he would be the first to tell Percy to back off if he got too clingy.

"How did we ever get to be friends?"

The question popped out of his mouth, and he cringed inside. Just because he was starting to rethink his friendship with Alden didn't mean that he should be talking aloud about it.

"Why? Because a snobbish Gypsy and a regular old Beasor shouldn't be friends?"

The laughter in Alden's voice told Percy his friend was teasing, but it was kind of what Percy meant.

"Well, yeah. I mean we really shouldn't be hanging out—or even living together," he pointed out.

"True, but we have your family to thank for you moving in with me, Percy. If they weren't so annoying and horrid to you, you'd still be living at their compound." Alden ran his hand over Percy's hair.

Percy shivered at Alden's touch. Alden tugged a blanket off the back of the couch, and tucked it around Percy, taking care of him. He realised Alden thought he was cold. Percy hadn't figured out a way to broach the subject of his attraction to Alden.

It'd been growing for several months now, and, while he was afraid it might ruin their friendship if Alden didn't feel the same way, Percy knew it would be coming to a head some point soon. Percy had never been known for keeping his mouth shut, and every time Alden touched him the desire grew stronger.

One day soon, he was going to throw himself into Alden's arms, and kiss the man senseless. Percy really hoped it wouldn't ruin anything.

"We're friends because I can deal with all your little quirks and inherent snobbiness. All of it stems from how you were raised, and you're getting better at accepting others who aren't nearly as beautiful or talented as you are." Alden chuckled. "I'm here to remind you there's a big world out there, and you need to start seeing more of it. If you'd stayed with your family, you would have lost touch with the rest of society."

Percy nodded, rubbing his cheek over Alden's shirt. "You're right. I don't think my parents remember there are people outside the gates of our compound, unless those people can pay them for their talents."

"But you've always been curious, and you peeked your cute little nose out of your ivory tower to see how the peasants live. It was the best day of my life when I rescued a bedraggled young Gypsy, lost in the scary world of the regular folk."

Leaning back, Percy glared up at Alden. "I wasn't lost."

Alden lifted his eyebrows, and Percy huffed.

"All right. I was completely lost, and terrified. I clamped on to you as my saviour the minute I saw how all those other boys ran away from you." Percy shrugged, and tried to get out of Alden's embrace.

"Oh, no. Don't stomp off in a huff, honey. I know you'd probably have saved yourself, and you didn't really need my help to find your way back home, but how could I pass up a chance to be the hero for some rare creature who seemed to have fallen from the sky?"

Percy blinked, and stared at Alden for a moment. Was that how Alden had seen him? As some unusual being visiting the boring world Alden lived in? Percy had never heard Alden say anything like that.

"I'm not unique or beautiful, you know that. Hell, all of my siblings are far more beautiful than me. I'm rather plain for a Gypsy," he said, grimacing as he heard his parents' words issuing from his mouth.

Alden cupped Percy's face in his hands. Those marvellous hazel eyes of Alden's peered into his, and Percy feared Alden would see how much he really did love him. As much as Percy wanted to look away, he didn't, because there was something in Alden's eyes that he had never seen before.

His best friend was looking at him with longing buried deep in his gaze. Percy blinked, and whatever he had seen there was gone. It had to have been his own wishful thinking, because Alden could do so much better than a neurotic and selfish Gypsy whose own family didn't want him.

"I've met your family, Percy, and let me tell you something. I think they're jealous of you, because you are, by far, the most beautiful Gypsy I've ever seen." Alden pressed his finger to Percy's lips. "Before you argue with me, remember, I've even met the Chairman of the High Council, who is a Gypsy as well, and he can't hold a candle to you."

Percy managed to not roll his eyes at Alden's statement. He'd met the Chairman as well, and the man was otherworldly gorgeous. Percy knew he wasn't anywhere near that level of good-looking.

"I think you're a little biased." He winked, and Alden grinned.

"You might be right. I think the Chairman is a pompous ass, and he believes, like most of the magical Beasors, that he is far superior to us normal people. There's nothing attractive or sexy about arrogance." Alden tweaked Percy's nose.

Percy blushed, and frowned. Why was he blushing? Alden wasn't really calling him sexy or attractive, was he? He eased away far enough so he was no longer touching Alden, and he met Alden's questioning gaze.

"Why don't you have a boyfriend? Or someone you can spend time with?"

"I do have someone I can spend time with." Alden shook his head. "I have you, and I'm not looking for a boyfriend. I like my life the way it is."

"Are you sure? We aren't getting any older, and your birthday is coming up in a couple of days. I mean, if you meet someone and want to bring them back to the apartment, just let me know and I'll hang out in the bar or something."

If he could, he'd kick his own butt. Why was he shoving Alden into someone else's arms? It would tear his heart out to see Alden with a boyfriend, but, if Percy couldn't bring himself to say anything, he shouldn't expect Alden to always be there whenever Percy needed someone to take care of him.

A wrinkle marred Alden's forehead. "I know that, and I appreciate your willingness to help me get laid, but I'm happy with my life at the moment. If—or when—things change, I'll let you know."

Sighing, Percy pushed to his feet, and stretched. Alden coughed, and Percy shot a glance over at his friend. Alden was staring at Percy's stomach, revealed by the movement, and his shirt had ridden up. Percy thought he saw heat flaring in Alden's eyes for a second, before Alden lowered his gaze.

"Are you really happy, Alden?"

Alden stood, and encircled Percy's waist with a tight hug. "Yes, you worrywart. I'm perfectly happy with my life, and I'm not interested in doing anything different."

Percy rested his forehead on Alden's shoulder for a moment. He took a deep breath, and gave himself a stiff talking-to. He needed to get a hold of himself, think about what he wanted to do, and figure out a way to do it.

Chapter Two

Percy strolled into Alden's pub, and hit a wall of sound. It was packed as usual, and Percy smiled, knowing Alden would be thrilled. The pub had become the place where all Beasors could socialise without worrying about being bothered, which had increased Alden's business a hundredfold.

He nodded to Reagan as he made his way through the crowd. If he wanted, he could have had Reagan escort him to the bar, but he liked to mingle and see who had shown up on any given night.

"Percy!"

His name broke through the noise, and Percy turned to see Chal, one of Alden's friends, waving at him from a corner booth. As much as Percy wanted to go and say hello to Alden, he knew that it wouldn't upset his friend if he didn't head straight over.

"Hello, Chal. How are you tonight?" Percy stopped by the booth, propped his hip against the side, and looked over at the bar.

"I'm doing well. Getting ready to head out on a job. Thought I'd come have a couple drinks before taking off."

"Hmm."

Percy barely acknowledged Chal's comment. His gaze narrowed as a slender blond leaned on the bar, and fluttered his eyelashes at Alden. The sexy grin on Alden's face told Percy that his friend found the blond attractive. Percy clenched his hands as Alden stroked his fingers over the blond's arm.

"He loves you, you know."

Startled, Percy glanced down at Chal. "Who loves me?"

"Alden." Chal used his chin to point towards the bar.

"Sure he does. We're best friends. Aren't you supposed to love your best friend?"

Chal shook his head with a grunt. "You two are determined to be just friends. No, he loves you like a man loves the person he wants to spend all of his life with."

That statement caught Percy's attention, and he looked down at Chal.

"I don't think you know what you're talking about. If Alden loves me, why is he flirting with that little bit over there?" He tilted his head towards the blond.

The Tramp rolled his eyes. "I can see it because I would like Alden to look at me like he does you, but he never does. He might flirt with people, but have you seen him take any of them home?"

"No, but that doesn't mean he doesn't take them into the back room," Percy muttered. "Ow!"

Percy rubbed the spot where Chal had punched him. Chal grabbed his hand and jerked him down into the booth.

"Do you really think Alden would take some guy he just met into the back room? At which point did all your brain drain out of your head?" Chal shook his head. "It's like both of you are doing your damnedest to be unhappy, when all you have to do is talk to each other. Or better yet, don't talk. Just fuck, man."

Percy started to say something, but then Alden leaned over and kissed the blond on the cheek. Jealousy shot through him, and all he could think of was how he wanted to go over there and smack the smug look off the blond's face.

He shot to his feet, and Chal sighed.

"Where are you going?"

"I have to think about things. Need to decide if making a move is the right thing to do, or if I should just ignore how I feel, and let our friendship stay just that."

"Dude, just go over there, and lay a wet one on him. I guarantee you, Alden's not going to complain." Chal encouraged him by giving him a little shove towards Alden.

"No. I can't do this while running on emotions. I've done that too many times and had it blow up in my face. I don't want to lose Alden as a friend, so I need to make sure this is exactly what I want to do."

Percy turned and left the pub, heading up to their apartment. He settled on his bed in his room, and closed his eyes. He had to go somewhere else to think, and the first thought that hit his mind was to go to the human universe. He'd be able to find a place to hole up, and think things through before talking to Alden.

He meditated, and a tingling hit his fingers and toes. Flashing took a lot of power, leaving Percy vulnerable once he got to Earth. He had to hope he remembered the right location to land.

Things went black, and, the next thing Percy knew, he was leaning against a wall in the alley by a human bar. He wrinkled his nose at the stench. Before he could move and find someplace to rest, two men stepped out of the side door of the bar. He glanced up at them, and they grinned.

"What do we have here?"

Something in the speaker's tone told Percy he might be in trouble.

"What's a Gypsy doing out here? Shouldn't ya be back where ya come from? I didn't know they let ya wander around on ya'r own."

Shit! Humans weren't supposed to know who—or what—Gypsies were, but Percy thought he might be able to bluff his way out of it.

"Gypsy? What are you talking about?" He decided being belligerent might help.

The two men approached him, and he tried to straighten, but he still didn't have enough strength to do anything except watch them.

"Hey, Karl, ya got those ropes?" The man in charge gestured to the other guy.

"Sure. Thought ya were crazy when ya told me to carry them, but lookee here."

Percy shuddered at the sight of the ropes. No way did these humans know about silk and how magical Beasors were susceptible to it. He tried to fight as the men closed in, but he had no chance of getting away from them. He couldn't even use his power to call for help.

Karl grabbed Percy, holding him while the other man wrapped the ropes around Percy's wrists. His skin burned, and Percy bit back a moan as the silken bands got tighter.

"Looks like we got us a new pet, Karl. Let's go see what he can do."

With a jerk, the man forced Percy to follow him. This wasn't going to end well for Percy, and again acting without thinking had got him into trouble. Something told Percy he was going to miss Alden's birthday party the next night.

* * * *

Alden mingled with friends and long-time customers. He talked and joked, even having a shot or two with certain ones, but he kept his eyes open for Percy. In all the years he'd known the Gypsy, Percy had never missed his birthday. Even if Percy was on a job, he'd come and spend the day with Alden.

He'd seen Percy talking to Chal the night Percy had disappeared, but Chal hadn't been around either, so he couldn't even ask him about it. Had the Tramp said something to Percy to piss him off? Alden hadn't seen Percy leave, but he'd been busy turning some cute kid down.

It was Alden's thirty-seventh birthday, and he'd decided to talk to Percy later that night, after everyone had left. He was finally going to tell Percy how much he loved him—as more than just a friend. His nerves sparked the entire night while he waited for Percy to make an appearance.

After the party ended, and all the people went home, Alden shut off the lights in the pub before heading up to his apartment. He dropped onto the couch, covering his face with his hands and sighing. He must have upset Percy, and his friend was pouting somewhere. It was unusual for Percy to punish Alden this way. Percy treated a lot of people like they didn't mean anything to him, but he'd never missed Alden's birthday, and Alden was beginning to wonder if something had stopped Percy from coming.

He yawned, but didn't want to go to bed yet. Maybe Percy would show up later on, and Alden wanted to be up when he got home. As the night rolled on, Alden's eyes slowly dipped closed, and he drifted asleep.

The next day, when Percy still hadn't made an appearance by the time Alden woke up, Alden really started to worry. Even during Percy's worst temper tantrums, his friend hadn't gone this long without letting Alden know where he was, and if he was all right.

Swallowing his distaste, Alden phoned Percy's parents' house.

"Harlow residence," someone answered.

"Umm…I'd like to speak with Mr Harlow, please."

"May I ask who's calling?" The voice wasn't familiar, but the Harlows had a high turnover rate with their employees, so it didn't surprise Alden.

"It's Alden Sparks. I need to talk to him about his son, Percy."

"Certainly. I'll see if he's available."

Alden was put on hold, and he knew Percy's father wouldn't be available. After staying on the line for thirty minutes, Alden disconnected and dialled Percy's sister's personal phone. While Percy didn't have a great relationship with his family, Kiki, his sister, was Percy's favourite.

She cared about Percy in her own way. Alden figured, if she didn't know where Percy was, she could find someone who might. At least she could ask the Head Councilman for the Gypsies. If Percy was working a job, the Councilman would have approved it.

"Yes?"

"Kiki, it's Alden. I'm sorry to bother you, but it's about Percy." He spoke quickly, not wanting Kiki to hang up on him.

"Alden?"

"Yes, I'm a friend of Percy's."

Silence drifted over the line while Kiki probably tried to place Alden in her sphere of people.

"Oh, right. You own a restaurant or something. Percy rents a room from you or whatever." Kiki sounded proud of herself for remembering.

Alden rolled his eyes. "Kiki, you know who I am. Cut the bullshit. I need to know if you've seen Percy lately."

"Well, there's no need to be rude." Kiki huffed in annoyance.

"Listen, Kiki. I haven't seen or heard from Percy in three days. I need to know if he's on a job or something."

Kiki hummed as she thought. "That is weird. I might not talk to him for months, but he'd never go more than two hours without talking to you. He's unnaturally attached to you."

Alden's concern started to grow into something stronger.

"Kiki, can you find out if Percy had a confidential job or something? I'll have my friends look for him on my end," Alden suggested.

"Of course I will. I know Percy thinks we don't care about him, but we do. If something's wrong, and you—or Percy—need our help, please ask."

Alden wondered what Kiki wanted or needed, because she was being so cooperative, but at that moment he didn't care. He'd give her anything—and everything—she wanted if she came through for him.

"I'll owe you one, Kiki. Thanks." He hung up before she said anything else.

With nowhere else to look and no one else to call, Alden went downstairs. Hopefully, working at the bar would help ease his mind away from obsessing about Percy's absence.

As the night progressed, Alden was able to let the customers move Percy to the back of his mind. Yet Percy never left his thoughts, and Alden couldn't shake the feeling that he was in trouble.

Chal came in around midnight. The Tramp looked tired, and Alden poured him a mug of ale without Chal asking. Chal propped his elbows on the bar before taking a big swig of his drink.

"Been busy?"

"No rest for the wicked or the weary," Chal joked. "I've been travelling between the universes like crazy this week. I wish there were other ways for you normal Beasors to get your stuff."

Alden snorted. "You Tramps have spoiled us. If the Tramp who discovered he could do it had just kept his mouth shut, you wouldn't be worked to the bone."

"True. Damn that man." Chal shoved his empty mug across the bar at Alden. "Sorry I missed your birthday. What crazy thing did Percy get you this year?"

"I don't know. He didn't show up." Alden shrugged. "In fact, I haven't seen him for three days. I have no idea where the bloody hell the bastard is."

Frowning, Chal straightened from the bar. "Really? You have no idea where Percy is?"

"No. If I did, I'd go and beat his ass for making me worry like this. He's never left without at least letting me know where he was going, and when he'd be back."

"I know. It's like you're an old married couple or something, without the sex, though, because you won't get off your cowardly ass and tell the Gypsy how you feel about him."

Alden whirled to glare at the Tramp. "Chal, I don't want to hear your opinions on my personal life. At the moment, I just want to find Percy. I can't help thinking there's something wrong, and he can't come home."

Chal studied Alden with a narrowed gaze. "You're really worried about him."

"Yes. It might seem silly or whatever, but I keep getting the feeling he's in trouble, and I need to find him. I don't think he's anywhere in this universe, or someone would have seen him. If he's gone to one of the other universes, I can't go and save him." Alden bit his lip, trying to get a hold of his emotions.

He didn't know what he would do if Percy never came back. For most of his life, Alden's entire universe had revolved around one slightly self-centred Gypsy, and Alden was all right with that. Something would be broken inside him without Percy around to brighten his life.

"Take a deep breath, dude. Let me get some sleep. Tomorrow, I'll start talking to some of my Tramp friends. Maybe they've heard or know something. Do you have someone talking to the other Gypsies?"

Alden nodded. "Yes. Kiki, Percy's sister, is looking into that for me. Do you know any Thieves?"

Chal shook his head. "No way. I try to avoid those pricks as much as possible."

"Maybe I could be of service."

The softly spoken words brought both Alden's and Chal's gazes around to see a diminutive man, standing next to the Tramp. His gold eyes gleamed in the shadowy bar, his black curls barely contained under a red cotton scarf.

"If you're trying to blend in, you're failing," Chal pointed out to the Thief.

"I know. I suck at this, but I couldn't stand being at the Council facility any longer. If I hear one more person try to convince me stealing is okay, I'll scream." The Thief looked at them with a slight smile. "My name is Steril, and I'm sorry to acknowledge that I was eavesdropping, but, if you need someone to ask around the Thieves community, I'd like to help."

Alden studied Steril, who barely looked old enough to be in the bar. There was an innocence in Steril's gaze that Alden didn't normally see in the eyes of a Thief. Whether he trusted Steril or not didn't matter at that moment. What mattered was finding Percy and kicking his friend's ass when he did.

"Are you even old enough to be in here? If you could do it discreetly, I'd appreciate it. I'm looking for Percy Harlow. He's a Gypsy, and my best friend. He's been missing for three days, and I'm worried about him."

Steril nodded, but stared at Alden. "Yes, I'm probably as old as you are. I just look young. And Gypsies tend to be flighty creatures. Are you sure he didn't just go off somewhere and forget to tell you he was going?"

As much as Alden wanted to yell at Steril, he realised that the Thief didn't know either of them. Steril didn't know how strong their friendship was. Alden took a deep breath.

"I know Gypsies are flighty, and Percy can be the worst of the bunch, but not to me. He might forget to tell everyone else, but he never forgets about me."

"Are you lovers?" There was nothing but curiosity in Steril's voice.

Beasors accepted all kinds of sexual pairings, though some of the older generations didn't understand and tended to be disgusted by same-sex couples. Those raised at the Council's facilities leaned towards disapproval as well.

"No. We're best friends," Alden said.

Chal burst out laughing. "They're best friends, because Alden can't grow a pair big enough to tell Percy he loves him. If we get Percy back, and you hang around the bar, you'll see it. I'm shocked Percy hasn't figured it out yet."

Alden wanted to reach across the bar and punch Chal in the face. He didn't have a lot of nerves left, but Chal was getting on his last ones. He clenched his hands, crushing the towel he held.

"Well, I don't really care one way or the other if you are lovers," Steril admitted. "It's none of my business either. I just wanted to make sure this Percy really would make sure you knew what he was doing. I guess if you're as good friends as you say, then he'd have tried to get a hold of you."

"Yes, and he hasn't for three days," Alden pointed out.

"Yes. I heard that part. Well, I heard everything, and, to be honest, I think you might be right to panic, sir." Steril didn't look happy to be reporting that.

"Oh, I'm Alden and this is Chal." Alden finally remembered to introduce himself and the Tramp.

"I knew who you were, Alden. I've been in here before, just never talked to anyone. Not that anyone would want to talk to a Thief. I don't steal just because I can. I don't think stealing is right, even if I have the power to do so." Steril ran out of energy and his babbled words stopped running over each other.

"Steril, there's a reason why my bar is so popular with all Beasors. I don't discriminate against anyone, and no one messes around in here, or they're banned." Alden wanted to wrap Steril up in a big hug. It sounded like the little Thief had some issues.

"Oh, I know. That's why I came in here. I might be a Thief, but I'm not very big, so, if someone wanted to start something with me, they could do some damage. At least in here I'm protected, for the most part." Steril grimaced as something buzzed on his person. "That's my phone. It's probably my dad or my teacher at the facility wondering where I am. I have to go, but I'll do some checking for you, Alden, and get back to you tomorrow."

Alden rushed around the bar, and swept Steril up in a huge hug. "Thank you so much, Steril. Drinks are on me, and, if you ever need any help, please let me know."

Steril squeaked in surprise, but the bright smile on his face when Alden set him back down told Alden he didn't mind the hug at all.

"I haven't done anything for you, and I might not have any news when I come back," Steril warned.

"I know, but you're trying to help someone you don't even know. Percy will appreciate it, and he'll tell you that when we find him and drag his ass back here." Alden patted Steril on the shoulder.

The Thief threaded his way through the crowd and out of the door. Alden went back to his side of the bar and poured out another mug for Chal. The Tramp slammed back the ale and set the mug on the bar.

"I'm going to get some sleep. If I find out anything, I'll come by tomorrow night." Chal nodded at him before leaving.

Alden rinsed out a few glasses, before he couldn't deal with it anymore. He let Greta know he was going back up to his apartment. He locked his door behind him, and slid to the floor, head in his hands.

"Where the hell are you, Percy? Why'd you leave without telling me where you were going? What am I going to do if you never come back?"

* * * *

Why had he flashed to Earth without telling someone? Even though he'd been angry with Alden for flirting with that little slut, he could have told Reagan or Greta before he'd left. When was he going to start thinking before he did shit?

Percy tugged on the silken ropes tying his wrists to the headboard of the bed. He winced as pain rippled through him. It wasn't just from the uncomfortable position he lay in. He ached from using his powers to help the stupid humans win at the racetrack, and from the almost non-stop sex they forced him to have when they returned from said track.

Being a Gypsy, Percy was highly sexual. He loved the sounds and smells of sex, and it helped him replenish his powers by having it. Yet the humans weren't allowing him the time to restore his power. They fucked him, and crawled back under whatever rock they had come from.

He rested his head on the pillow under him, and grimaced. God, he wished they'd let him take a shower or clean up somehow. He stank, and his skin felt like he hadn't been clean in weeks. How long had they kept him in the dark room? Percy'd lost track of time after the second day he'd been tied up.

What perverse god would make silk the bane of Beasors everywhere? Such a beautiful material, yet Percy couldn't use his ability to flash back to Beasor because of the silk. It put him under their control, and he hated it.

Poor Alden was probably out of his mind with worry by now. Percy had the feeling he'd missed Alden's birthday. *I haven't done that since we met.* He hoped Alden wasn't angry with him.

Actually, Percy had a feeling Alden was searching for him, but, because Percy was a complete idiot, Alden had no idea he needed to come to Earth to find him. Percy bit his lip to keep from breaking down into sobs. He'd give up all his powers to be able to tell Alden he loved him as far more than his best friend. If he ever got free from this prison, and could look Alden in the eye, he'd spill his guts. Percy would do his damnedest to convince Alden to give their relationship a shot.

The creak of the door opening warned Percy, and he took a deep breath. He'd never cried or shouted while the men screwed him. There was no point in voicing his displeasure or hurt. It didn't stop them from doing it, but it meant he got to keep his pride.

"See, I told ya we got one of them Gypsies," Karl, one of his captors, spoke up.

Percy kept his gaze on the ceiling. He didn't care to look into the empty eyes of the humans who used him. It was easier to think of them as monsters, than the pathetically ordinary men they were.

A soft gasp surprised him and he dropped his gaze to the men standing in the doorway. The young man with Karl stared at Percy like he'd seen a ghost. Percy didn't recognise the lad, but it didn't mean anything. If the boy knew what Percy was, he'd more than likely want him as well. It wasn't arrogance making Percy think that. It was some sort of sickness humans had. If they saw a Gypsy, they wanted him or her.

"Do ya want to fuck him? He's not too bad. Getting skinny, though. Almost like fucking a bag of bones." Karl spat.

Percy lifted his gaze back up, not wanting to see the kid's agreement. Shock raced through him when the kid didn't beg to take him.

"No, Karl. I hafta go." The kid sounded sick.

"Whaddya mean ya hafta go? Ya just got here. We got beer and shit. The Gypsy helped us win at the track again," Karl protested.

"I just remembered an appointment I got. I can't stay."

The door shut, and Percy couldn't help but heave a slight sigh of relief. At least that was one fewer person who'd be fucking him that night. Each time it happened, he could feel a little more of his soul leaving. His power was slowly draining away, and he couldn't do anything to replenish it, because Karl and his partner were using him too fast.

For the first time in the darkness, Percy conceded the fact that he was probably going to die on Earth, tethered to some kind of hellhole where he'd fade away. His heart broke because he knew Alden would be devastated when Percy didn't come back. Alden had many friends, but none of them as close to him as Percy was.

Wetness leaked from the corners of Percy's eyes as he thought about all the good times he and Alden had had together. All the times he'd spent curled up in Alden's arms, chatting away about his day or what job he was working. How many times had Alden let him talk without ever complaining or trying to talk about himself? Alden had been the only person Percy knew who hadn't wanted anything from Percy, except his friendship.

The only time Alden had ever asked Percy to use his powers was to keep mice out of the bar, so it really wasn't for his own personal gain, and he'd never thought that, just because Percy was a Gypsy, it meant that Percy was easy. Oh, there were times when Percy had caught Alden staring at him like Percy was a particularly yummy piece of candy, and Alden had a really bad sweet tooth. Yet Alden had never acted on his desire, and maybe it was because Alden didn't want to ruin their friendship by asking for something for himself.

Percy knew he shouldn't be thinking about Alden, because it just made the entire situation harder to deal with, and yet it made it all a little easier as well. When Karl and Roscoe came to Percy, he went into a different reality where he and Alden were in love and each touch was Alden's. Somewhere in his mind, he knew it wasn't Alden, because his friend would never touch him so roughly or hurt him in any way. Yet, to keep from going crazy, Percy took himself to that place and allowed Alden to keep him safe.

The door creaked again, and Percy tensed, figuring it would be Karl or Roscoe coming back for the first of many fucks. Yet the steps across the wooden floor were lighter, and somehow they managed to sound stealthy, like the person making them didn't want anyone to hear.

A presence stood next to his bed, and Percy couldn't fight the need to see who it was. He peered to his right, and blinked in surprise at the sight of the kid standing there. The kid glanced over his shoulder back at the door for a second before looking back at Percy.

"Who are you?"

Percy frowned, unsure why that would be important. "My name is Percy Harlow."

"Oh, shit," the kid muttered. "I'm going to try to get you out of here. I can't do it myself, or else it won't work. They don't trust me alone long enough for me to free you, but I know who I can tell about you. Someone will be coming to help you. Is there someone you want to know where you are?"

"Alden Sparks," Percy whispered. "Tell them to tell Alden about me, and he'll come to get me."

Percy didn't know how Alden would do it, but he knew, once Alden discovered where Percy was, Alden would move all the universes to get to him.

A door slamming shut somewhere in the house caused the kid to jump. He patted Percy on the arm.

"I wish I could help you now, but I can't. I'll tell them to tell Alden about you. That's the best I can do."

"I understand. Thank you." Percy pointed to the door with his chin. "Get out of here, or they'll do something to you."

The kid nodded, and scurried out of the room like he was in danger of catching something. Percy let his eyes close, and his heart soar. He had to believe the kid was telling the truth and would get him help.

As the door opened a third time, and the stench of unwashed bodies hit him, Percy calmed his heart. He could last however long it took for Alden to come for him. He'd never let go of the conviction that Alden would save him.

Chapter Three

A day or two later, as the door opened once more, Percy cringed, knowing that whoever was walking into the room wasn't friendly.

"Let's go, Gypsy. We're heading out to the track again, and you're going to work your magic on some horses for us."

Percy bit back his cry of pain as Roscoe tried to jerk him to his feet without untying Percy's wrists from the headboard. Roscoe had done the same thing several times, so Percy should have been used to it by then.

"Fucking Karl," Roscoe muttered. "I told him there ain't no point in keeping ya tied up. Ya ain't getting outta the room as long as we got silk on ya."

Percy had been trying to figure out how Roscoe and Karl, two of the least intelligent humans he'd run into, knew about the Beasors' allergy to silk. How did they know anything about Beasors and what they could do?

He'd never got around to asking them, not that they would have answered him anyway. He'd met a few humans who had made contact with Beasors before, but the humans had never known all of the Beasors' secrets.

"Ya got the pretty dude?" Karl stood by the front door of the house.

Percy never got a chance to look around the place. Roscoe and Karl hustled him out into the truck, and tossed him on the back seat. He grunted as his shoulders hit the opposite door. It sucked not having his hands to keep his balance, or stop from crashing into things.

"Keep ya head down. Don't want no one to see ya."

The humans climbed into the front of the truck, and they sped away from the kerb. Percy rose just a little bit to peek out of the window. He wanted to see where he was, just in case he got away. He hadn't seen the kid since the moment he'd promised to let someone know where he was.

Was the kid truly going to help him? How much more could he take before his body gave out? It wasn't just the almost constant sex Roscoe and Karl put him through. It was how they dragged him to the track every day until the track closed. They made him talk to every horse scheduled to run in every race that day.

He wasn't given any chance to recharge. If they were only having sex with him once a night, and he was willing, Percy could have replenished his power. Also, if they had taken off the silk ropes holding him captive, his power wouldn't have disappeared so fast. But constant use had drained his reserves, and he was losing strength as the hours went by.

Dropping back down to the floor, he curled in a foetal position and closed his eyes. At least in the truck he could feel the sun and warmth, though in the human universe the light was far dimmer than from Beasor's stars.

Percy sneezed as the exhaust fumes blowing in through Karl's open window hit his nose. While there were many things Percy liked about the human universe, and especially Earth, he didn't like the smells of the vehicles that burned gas. On Beasor they used electric hover sleds, and, because their sun was so bright, most of their vehicles and power was generated by solar energy and wind.

No pollution of any kind kept their planet clean, and Beasor was the shining jewel of their universe. Percy missed his room in Alden's apartment. He missed his bed, and hanging out in Alden's bar with friends, while his best friend poured drinks.

He bounced his forehead off the floor with a snort. *What kind of idiot flashes to another universe without telling anyone? What kind of idiot would run away instead of staying around to see what was going on between Alden and that blond Beasor?*

Percy trembled, and imaged Alden sitting with him. He smiled at how ordinary Alden looked, with his brown hair and hazel eyes. Like every other Beasor who didn't have any magic, Alden shone with his own brightness. While most magical Beasors would ignore Alden, Percy had seen Alden's soul in the way the man looked at him.

He was used to being the centre of attention for most Beasors, simply because of his good looks, he understood that true beauty wasn't just on the outside. The day he'd met Alden had turned out to be the best day of his life.

He'd left his family's compound when he was twenty, determined to make it on his own instead of coasting along on his family's reputation. His father had wanted to create a dynasty of Gypsies, using his family to control nature, and getting paid by rich Beasors to make their businesses profitable.

Percy didn't want to use his powers simply for profit. In fact, he would have preferred to live like Alden, without worrying about magic or how others might want to use him. He'd left home and found himself homeless on the street. Percy hadn't eaten for days, and hadn't got any jobs. He suspected his father had put out the word on hiring him, and the Head Gypsy on the High Council was a friend of Percy's father.

Alden was only two years older than Percy, but he'd been on his own for a couple of years. He managed a bar in downtown Catalai then, and offered Percy a place to crash until Percy found a job and a place to stay. It had been over fifteen years since then, and Alden had never once told Percy to leave.

Percy had started getting jobs shortly after moving in with Alden, and he'd paid his half of the bills, even though Alden'd never asked for it. Fifteen years had helped build their friendship into something more. Percy had just never been willing to go the extra step because he wanted to keep their friendship on an even keel.

The truck stopped and Percy took a deep breath, opened his eyes, and waited. The doors opened, and he listened as Karl and Roscoe climbed out of the vehicle.

"Get out now, Gypsy."

He grimaced as Roscoe grabbed his arm, and yanked him from the back seat. Percy wrinkled his nose at the gasoline stench from the cars parked alongside Karl's truck. The noise of people talking and laughing while walking into the clubhouse for the track exploded in his ears. Percy always returned to his room with a pounding headache.

Karl used his work ID to get them in and to the backstretch where the horses were stabled. Roscoe escorted them, not saying much to anyone, while Karl nodded to people he knew. Percy had gone through this routine several times since they'd captured him.

"Now this horse is the odds-on favourite to win the first race today." Roscoe kept his voice low as they walked up to the first stall. "We don't want him to win. He needs to come in second. We're placing a bet on the horse you'll be talking to next."

Karl nudged Percy closer to the stall, and the horse hung its head over the door. Percy stared into the beast's eyes, and slowly put images into the horse's mind. He spoke, in images, of the horse coming in second behind the first one. The horse snorted and bobbed its head up and down.

"It's done." Percy stumbled as his vision blurred. Weakness made his head swim, and all he wanted was to find somewhere to curl up and sleep.

"Good. Only about thirty more to go." Karl laughed cruelly.

"Oh, lucky me," Percy muttered.

"What did ya say?" Roscoe jerked on the silk wrapped around Percy's wrist, bringing him closer to the human. "Ya not talking back, are ya? 'Cause that might not be the smartest thing I've heard ya do."

Percy rolled his eyes. "What are you going to do to me? It isn't like you haven't already done everything possible to me, and it's not like I can get away from you."

He held up his hands to show off the bands of silk around his wrists. Roscoe shoved them down while looking around to make sure no one had seen them.

Percy had learnt never to talk to anyone else while they were out. By their appearance and attitude, Roscoe and Karl tended to intimidate people, and Percy didn't want to risk hurting innocent humans.

"We could do a lot worse than we have. Trust us, Gypsy. We could invite some of our friends over to have a go at ya. I bet ya'd enjoy that." Karl leered at him.

Percy gagged on the horrid stench of Karl's breath. He wanted to push the human away, but didn't think he had the strength to do that plus keep standing. He turned his head to the side, and caught a young man staring at him. Something in the way the kid looked at him hinted at knowledge of what Percy was, and what the humans were doing. Percy looked a little closer, and realised it was the kid from the other day.

"Come on. We got lots of horses to see, and then make our bets. If ya do good today, pretty, we just might let ya take a shower when we get home. Of course, one of us will have to be in there with ya. Can't take a risk of letting the cash cow get away."

Roscoe led the way to the next stall, and on and on until Percy's brain blurred with all the horses. He didn't remember much after using his power to get the last horse to do as he said. They went to the grandstands, and sat. Karl stayed with him while Roscoe placed their bets. All Percy wanted was to eat and sleep, but he wouldn't be able to do that. Sometimes, if things were going well at the horse track, one of the humans would take him over to the dog track and get him to rig those as well.

"You know someone's going to catch on to you two eventually. You can't have a winning ticket in every race on every day. The odds are stacked against you, even if you understood horses, which you two obviously don't." Percy felt the need to point it out to Karl.

"I doubt they're smart enough to figure out what we're doing." Karl shrugged, looking down at the racing programme. "If they do, we'll hightail it outta here, and find somewhere else to set up shop."

Unfortunately, Percy could see what the next months of his life would be like, if Alden didn't find him. Yet he also knew he wouldn't last much more than a couple of months because already he had to work harder and harder to get his magic to work.

"How did you know what I was?" He'd asked before, but neither man had seemed interested in answering.

"Oh, we'd caught one of ya before. Saw her pop outta thin air, and we grabbed her."

Percy's stomach dropped at the thought of one of his fellow Gypsies at the mercy of Roscoe and Karl. For it to have been a female Gypsy made it all that much worse. Percy could tell he was slowly reaching the end of his sanity, but he imagined it had been twice as bad for a woman.

"Figured out silk keeps ya under control, and what kinda power ya'll got over animals. Roscoe figured out if we could get our hands on another of ya, we could make money at the track." Karl shrugged. "Seems to be working."

"What happened to the first one you kidnapped?" Percy didn't really want to know the answer, but he thought he'd ask.

"We dumped her body in the swamp. Didn't last long. Maybe two weeks or so. Good thing we grabbed us a guy this time. You're tougher than she was." Karl kicked Percy's leg. "Making us more money than she did, too."

"Well, bully for me," Percy muttered, wishing he could jerk free of Karl's grip and run away, but there wasn't any way he'd get his legs to carry him more than ten feet before Karl caught him again.

"Shut it. The first race is about to go off."

Karl turned to face the track, and Percy leant back against the bench behind him. He let his head drop back and closed his eyes. It really wasn't resting or sleeping, because there was so much noise and too many smells competing to make his head ache. But, still, being able to close his eyes for a little while helped to build up enough energy so he could stay sitting up, instead of slipping into a puddle at Karl's feet.

The stale, sweat-scented air drifted over Percy's nose, and he cringed inside when Roscoe sat next to him. God, what he wouldn't do to have enough strength to get rid of both of them, but when had wishful thinking done anything for him since he'd got into this situation?

The clang of the starting gate opening clued Percy in to what was happening. He didn't need to watch, because he knew the outcome. None of the horses had ever let him down before, and, while his power had weakened, it still held sway over their animal minds. He slowed his breathing down, and slowly gathered the few strands of power he had left into the centre of his being.

Meditating at a racetrack was difficult because the noises and smells served as a distraction, but, when it was the only time he could do so out in the sunlight, Percy'd take what he could get. Sadness lingered in his heart when he noticed how weak his magic was.

He'd never got so low before, and he wasn't sure what he could do besides resting that would help build his reserves back up. Usually he'd have sex and the relaxing afterglow would be enough to strengthen what he'd lost during a job. Roscoe and Karl raping him didn't count as sex, which wasn't surprising since Percy needed to be calm and relaxed to meditate.

Suddenly his arms were jerked hard enough that Percy lost his balance and hit the bench beside him with his shoulder. He opened his eyes to glare at Roscoe, who sneered at him.

"Okay, I got it covered here. Karl's gonna take ya over to the dog track. Might be able to make some kinda dough off them mutts today."

Percy managed to push himself to his feet, and follow Karl without commenting. No point in arguing, because Percy had learnt he'd pay for it when they got back to the house.

"Hey, I been meaning to ask, how do ya jump from wherever ya come from?" Karl didn't look back at him while they made their way through the crowd.

"I don't know. I really don't think there's anyone in my universe that knows how we do what we do." Percy narrowed his eyes as he paused for a moment before continuing, "I guess one of the scientists at the High Council might have an idea, but, since I tend not to spend any time with them or at the Council compound, I wouldn't know."

Karl grunted, but didn't say anything else. They climbed into the truck, and this time Percy was allowed to ride in the front seat. *Just like a pet dog*, he thought, as he stared out of the window. When would Alden come and rescue him, for all his foolishness?

* * * *

48

From the barn where he'd hidden, Jackie watched Karl drive the Gypsy away from the track. They were probably headed to the dog track on the other side of town. Jackie shook his head. The poor guy looked like he was hanging on by a thread of determination. Maybe he really did believe that Jackie would be able to tell someone about him.

"Jackie, you ready to go?"

He looked up to see his boss coming towards him. Jackie nodded, and a tingle of excitement raced through him. Their next delivery would get him close to someone he could leave a message with. Then it would be up to that guy to pass it on.

Jackie couldn't risk Roscoe or Karl finding out what he planned on doing. They'd beat him to within an inch of his life, and probably toss him out of their house. It was the only place he had to crash at night, and he hated the dark, so he took a lot of punishment to ensure he wasn't out in it. Of course, he could leave at any time, but he wasn't finished with his mission yet.

They climbed in the truck, and headed to the club where they were delivering a couple of kegs of beer. He took one of the kegs off the truck and carted it into the back room of the bar. Jackie peeked into the front of the building, searching for the person he needed to talk with. He spotted her at the end of the counter.

Gathering his courage and straightening his shoulders, he walked over to her.

"Excuse me, ma'am. I wondered if I could talk to ya for a second. I won't take no more time than that."

The woman turned, her blonde braid swinging behind her. Jackie gasped as her lavender eyes met his. She was definitely the right person to talk to. The big guy she was talking with took a step towards

Jackie, and Jackie cowered, ducking his head down. He didn't want to get hit, but he really needed to talk to the woman.

"Simon, stop. Let him be." Her voice was soft and accented. "What did you want to talk to me about?"

Jackie didn't raise his gaze from the floor. He knew better than to look at her. "Umm…there's one of your kind caught here."

"My kind? Here? What do you mean caught here?" Her voice was sharp. An elegant hand came into Jackie's line of vision and lifted his chin. "Maybe you should look at me when we talk. It'll be easier for me to see if you're lying or not."

He blinked as their eyes met, and he took a deep breath.

"I know what ya are, ma'am. I know ya aren't from here. A guy who's from where ya's from is being held captive by a couple of guys I know. I couldn't get him free, but he told me to tell ya to go looking for Alden Sparks."

Her grip on Jackie's chin tightened. "Alden Sparks? Do you know the Gypsy's name?"

Jackie tried to nod his head, but he couldn't move because of her holding him. "Percy."

She let him go and patted him on the shoulder. "Shit, that sucks. Give me the address of where he's being held. I'll make sure the right people know about it."

He rattled off the address for Karl's house. As he finished, his boss stuck his head out of the back room.

"Jackie, what the fuck are you doing out there? You know you're supposed to stay back here or out with the truck." His boss gestured for him. "Get back here."

"Yes, sir." Jackie started to turn away, but whirled around to face the woman again. "Ya've got to hurry, ma'am. He ain't looking too good."

"Thank you, Jackie. I appreciate it, and I know all the people looking for the Gypsy will appreciate as well."

Nodding, Jackie left, not even listening to his boss yelling at him. He'd done something right in his life, and that was all that mattered.

Chapter Four

"Alden!" Chal shouted the moment he hit the door of the bar.

Alden glanced up to watch the Tramp shoving customers out of the way. Reagan headed towards Chal, but Alden caught his eye and shook his head. Normally, Chal was relatively polite, so Alden assumed that he had something important to share.

Excitement built inside him. Maybe the Tramp had news about Percy. His best friend had been missing for over a week now, and Alden had grown frustrated without any leads.

"Over here, Chal," Alden called to his friend, waving his hand to catch Chal's attention.

Chal wound his way quickly through the crowd, and dropped into the chair across the table from Alden. One of the waitresses delivered ale at about the same time. Alden nodded his thanks to Greta at the bar.

He waited while Chal took a drink and caught his breath. Chal swiped his hand over his mouth, and leant back in his chair.

"I came here as soon as I got some information," Chal announced.

"What news? Has someone found Percy?" Alden wanted to grab Chal and shake the Tramp until he spilled what he knew.

"Not necessarily found him, but I do know where he is. Unfortunately, he's being held captive in the human universe, and he's being used pretty badly. The way we know it's Percy is your name was mentioned specifically."

"Fuck." Alden slammed his fist onto the table. "We need to go get him."

"I know, man, which is why I'm here. I'll take you myself, though we have to be careful because two humans who seem to know something about Beasors are holding him. They have him tied with silk. Percy's not doing well, Alden."

Alden shoved to his feet, and gestured for Chal to follow him. He stopped by the bar.

"Greta, I'm leaving for the rest of the night. You and Reagan are going to have to handle things for a day or two. I'm not sure when I'll be back."

Greta reached over the bar, and gave Alden a one-arm hug. "Go get Percy back for us, boss."

"And beat the shit out of whoever hurt him," Reagan spoke up from where he stood next to the bar.

"We will. Thanks."

Alden led the way up to his apartment. He changed out of his work clothes into a pair of dark, tight pants and a tight shirt. Chal watched him with a frown.

"Are you thinking this is going to be a stealth mission? In and out?"

"Isn't it?" Alden looked through the door at Chal. "I thought we wouldn't want any other humans to know we were there."

Chal paused. "Actually it's going to be a snatch-and-grab mission for you. Your entire goal is to get Percy the hell out of there. Don't worry about the humans. Some friends of mine and I are going to teach them what happens when they mess with Beasors."

Alden wished he could help Chal teach the humans a lesson, but he was far more interested in getting Percy back. He wasn't looking forward to seeing how badly his friend was hurt, though, and he knew he'd have to control his own anger.

"All right. I'm ready to go." He tucked a knife in the top of his boot. He'd need something to cut the silk off. He wasn't nearly as incapacitated as the magical Beasors were by silk, but it still could weaken him if he touched it. Far easier just to cut it with a blade.

He walked out into the living room where Chal stood, arms folded and foot tapping on the floor. Alden went right up to Chal, and the Tramp wrapped a hand around his arm.

"Have you ever flashed before?"

Alden shook his head. "Never had any reason to, and you're the only Tramp I trust enough to give myself over to like this."

Flashing through the different universes was something all the magical Beasors could do without too much difficulty, though only Tramps could travel without losing any strength or power. Ordinary Beasors didn't have trouble with passing to other universes, but they didn't have any powers, so they needed Tramps to take them, since Tramps didn't lose power when they flashed.

No one could really explain what happened when a person flashed between the universes. He wondered whether a person disintegrated, then reappeared in whatever universe they wanted. How did the energy figure out where the Beasor wanted to go? Why were the Beasors the only ones in all the universes who could travel between them?

Alden had never travelled between the universes. While he wondered what the other worlds were like, he'd never felt the urge to see them. Also, if he flashed with a Tramp, he had to trust that the Beasor would take him exactly where he wanted to go. Alden didn't want to get stranded in some world he didn't know anything about.

"Trust me, Alden. I wouldn't leave you because I love your bar, and it wouldn't be the same without you." Chal's grin seemed rather snarky. "It doesn't hurt, I can tell you that."

Alden shrugged. "I don't care if it tears out my fingernails—or anything like that. I just want to go to Percy and save him. I want him back here, in our apartment, with me."

Chal nodded. "I get that, but I have to warn you. He might not be in good shape when we find him. Do you have a doctor who can check him out when we get back?"

"I don't, but I'm sure Kiki can find one of the Gypsy doctors for me." Alden scowled at the thought of having to ask Kiki for another favour. "I'll worry about that later as well. I owe you big time for this, Chal."

"Of course you do, and, maybe someday, I'll claim that favour." Chal tightened his grip. "Close your eyes. It's a little tingling sensation, and then you'll feel nothing until we get to the human universe."

"Okay."

Alden closed his eyes, and, like Chal had said, the tingling started in his hands and feet. But within seconds there was nothing. Alden didn't know the exact moment they'd flashed or how long they'd spent in between universes. Everything ended for him until his body hit something solid with a thud, and air burst from his lungs.

"Ow!"

Opening his eyes, he looked to see Chal standing up and rubbing his butt. The Tramp glanced around in annoyance.

"I hate when I don't land right. Always makes me feel like an amateur," Chal muttered, before coming over to Alden. "Let me help you up."

Alden took Chal's offered hand, and allowed the Tramp to lift him to his feet. "Are we on Earth?"

He looked around. Nothing looked much different from Beasor, except that it seemed darker.

"Yes."

"Why would anyone want to live here—or even come visit here?"

"I don't know. Follow me."

As Alden followed Chal out of the stand of trees they'd landed in, he looked around. People were strolling down sidewalks, and large four-wheeled vehicles lumbered by in streams of foul-smelling exhaust. Those were cars. Alden remembered Percy telling him about them after his friend had come back from doing a job on Earth.

"Is it night-time here?" he asked Chal quietly, as they threaded their way through the people.

"No. Why?"

"It's so dark," he murmured.

Chal pointed at the buildings. "It's because their buildings tend to block out the sun."

Alden stopped and stared at the towering buildings surrounding them. They were several floors, and seemed created from glass and some kind of metal. On

Beasor, their structures were no taller than three floors at the most. Only the High Council's facilities were taller, and that was because they often housed visiting dignitaries and held the annual meetings for the Gypsies, Tramps and Thieves.

"Hey, don't stop in the middle of the sidewalk, idiot." A human ran into him, and shoved him out of the way.

Alden stumbled, but Chal caught him.

"Quit gawking. We don't have time to sightsee. We have to find the house where Percy is being held. I have an address." Chal led him away from the crowded streets and down towards other houses where Alden assumed humans lived, instead of worked.

"Do we know anything about who has Percy?"

Chal whistled softly while they walked. "It's two guys, and it sounds like they've been using Percy's power over animals to win money at the racetrack. They have him talk to the horses, I guess. Also, they've been fucking him without giving him a break. The person who got us the news about him said he looked like he didn't have much longer to live."

"I didn't think humans knew about Gypsies, or any other Beasors, for that matter. How did these two know what to use Percy for? And how did the other one know how to get a hold of someone to save Percy?" Confusion rippled through Alden.

Of course, he'd never had any contact with any other race aside from Beasors. He didn't understand human motives or reasoning. Maybe all of them would steal a Gypsy and use up his power, like Percy's captors were doing.

"I don't know. I'm just glad the human who gave us the information about Percy knew what he was, and whom to get the message to, or else we'd still be searching. There are millions of universes out there, and Percy could have gone to any one of them." Chal shook his head. "I wonder why he came here, though. The human universe isn't my favourite place to visit. I only tend to come here when I have a job."

Alden shrugged. "I don't know. Percy never said anything about liking to come here. Of course, there have been a few jobs he couldn't tell me about."

Chal stopped in front of a run-down house, and Alden scrunched his nose in disgust at the garbage surrounding the building. Paint peeled off the siding, and the front porch sagged in the middle. Percy had to be held captive there, because he would never have been caught dead visiting the place.

"What should we do?" Alden propped his fists on his hips while studying the structure.

"Let me go up and see if anyone's home. If no one's there, we'll break in and see if we can grab Percy. If someone is there, we'll figure something else out." Chal started to walk up towards the house.

"Wait, Chal."

They turned to see four more Tramps stroll up the sidewalk to join them. Alden didn't know them by their names, though he'd often seen them at his bar. Chal shook hands with all of them.

"Alden, these are my friends. They're going to hang around after I flash you and Percy back to Beasor. When I get back, we'll teach the humans what happens when you mess with Beasors."

Chal introduced the Tramps, and Alden nodded at them.

"I appreciate you coming. You guys can have free drinks for life at my bar," Alden promised.

"We thank you, but we don't need any free drinks. We're paying Chal back for favours he did us," the biggest Tramp said. "We already checked the place out. No one's home. Visi talked to the neighbours. We know which racetrack the humans go to, if you want to grab the Gypsy there."

Chal glanced back at Alden. "Ultimately this is your show, Alden. Do you want to wait for them to come back or do we go find Percy?"

"We go find Percy. If they're using him without giving him a chance to replenish, waiting even a few extra hours could kill him." Alden clenched his hands at the thought of his best friend dying because of someone else's selfishness. He didn't want to think about how empty his life would be without Percy.

"Okay. Let's go. We have a vehicle, since it's going to take us a little time to get to the track." Visi, one of the shorter Tramps, gestured towards a large black vehicle parked at the kerb.

Alden and his gang piled into the vehicle and Visi started it. They pulled into traffic, but Alden closed his eyes. He had never been in a car, and, if they hadn't needed to use it to save Percy, he wouldn't have got into it.

Chal bumped his shoulder, and Alden peeked at him.

"Don't worry. Visi has been driving for a while now. It was something he wanted to learn, and he enjoys it. In fact, most of these Tramps like hanging out here in the human universe."

"Why? I've only been here for an hour or so, and I already know I don't like it here." Alden closed his eyes again as they raced around a corner, but he opened them wide as Visi slammed on the brakes.

"What's not to like about this place?" the biggest Tramp asked, looking back from the front passenger seat.

"Your name was Digs, right?"

Digs nodded, and Alden gestured at the mass of people outside the vehicle.

"There are so many people, and how many of them know each other? It's obvious some of them are monsters. Just look at what they've done to Percy." Alden shuddered. "It's so dark here, even during the day."

Digs snorted. "We'll save your Gypsy friend, and you can go back to Beasor."

"I'll be happy to do so."

Alden wasn't going to argue with them about the merits of the human universe. He was simply trying to distract himself from the speed with which they were hurtling down the road by listing the things he didn't like about Earth. Of course, there weren't that many since it was the first time he'd been there.

Visi pulled into a place where hundreds of the human vehicles were parked. They stopped and Visi turned the machine off. After climbing out, Alden glanced around, and frowned.

"What is this place?"

"This is a track where they race horses like we have back home. The humans who have Percy bring him here every day, so they can fix the races. They use the Gypsy's power over the horses, and they bet on the ones they know will win." Digs frowned. "I'm sure they're not smart enough to hide what they're doing, so they might get into trouble soon. The humans have people who police things like that. Sort of like our High Council's security unit."

Alden nodded, but he didn't care about the humans. All he wanted was to find Percy, and take him home. "How do we find Percy?"

A throat-clearing cough caused them all to whirl around. A skinny young man stood there in threadbare clothes, and he shivered when all of them stared at him.

"Are you looking for the Gypsy?" His question was soft, like he didn't want anyone else to overhear him.

"Yes." Alden took a step towards the kid, but tried not to look threatening. "Can you tell me where to find him?"

"Follow me. It isn't right what they're doin' to him. He ain't lookin' good, either." The kid shook his head with sadness in his eyes. "The Gypsy's beautiful, but, if he don't get out of here, he's gonna die."

Alden couldn't help the growl issuing from his throat. The kid shot him a fearful glance.

"Don't worry, kid. Alden won't hurt you, but I wouldn't say the same if he gets his hands on the men who are holding his friend captive." Chal poked Alden in the side, and whispered under his breath, "Cool it. Don't scare the kid. He's our only hope to find Percy."

Alden dropped back, away from the kid. He didn't want to scare him either, but all he could think about was how alone Percy must feel, being used in every way possible by those monsters.

"How did you know what Percy was? And how did you know how to get a hold of someone who can help him?" Visi asked as they continued to walk.

"Karl and Roscoe, the guys that's got the Gypsy, knew what he was when they took him. I'm not sure how they know, but they got him tied with silk, and they don't leave him alone." The kid looked like he was about to cry. "I talked to some other people, and they said to talk to this girl. I don't know her name or nothing, just a bar to find her at. The Gypsy told me to use the name Alden Sparks, so I did."

"Does the Gypsy know you got a hold of us?"

"No." The human shook his head. "I couldn't get back in to see him without Karl or Roscoe. They would'a expected me to do stuff to him, and I don't want nothing to do with hurting people, even if they're aliens or whatever."

Alden wanted to protest the 'alien' comment. Beasors were no more aliens than humans were. They simply came from a different universe, and if humans were more intelligent or more evolved they would be able to see the other universes. Maybe some day humans would be able to travel among the universes, but, for now, they were stuck on their own planet. Alden couldn't imagine how narrow the humans' view of the universes was.

"I'm glad you were willing to take a chance, and help our friend out." Chal clapped the boy on the shoulder, and the kid almost fell over.

The kid shot Chal a look, and something in the kid's gaze told Alden he was far older, or had lived a rougher life, than Alden had thought.

"What's your name?" Alden wasn't sure why he'd asked. Maybe so he could know the man who'd saved Alden's love.

"I'm Jackie. Don't got a last name, 'cause I don't got any parents. Karl lets me hang around, and I do things for them. Nothing bad, 'cause I don't want to go to jail, but Karl and Roscoe are bad people." Jackie shrugged. "Ain't no one else willing to take me on."

Alden glanced over at Chal and Digs. Both Tramps nodded, and Alden realised they knew exactly what he was thinking. Jackie would find he had a new home and a job after this mission was done. Alden wasn't going to leave Jackie to the dubious mercies of Karl and Roscoe.

They all rounded the corner, and Jackie gestured towards a row of barns.

"Karl took the Gypsy to the third barn in that row. He makes him talk to the horses, tells them to win or lose, I guess. Not entirely sure how the whole thing works, ya know. But Roscoe will be around as well, so I can't be around here."

Alden stepped up and held out his hand. "I want to thank you, Jackie. What you did will save my friend's life, and it was truly courageous to help him."

Jackie ducked his head, but took Alden's hand in a firm shake. "I couldn't let Karl kill him, ya know. Nothing that pretty should be kept caged up."

"So true." Chal stepped forward. "Now get out of here. One of us will come see you after this is taken care of. You get a reward for helping us find him."

Jackie's eyes lit up at the mention of a reward, but Alden could tell the kid had done it because he'd truly thought Percy shouldn't be held captive.

The six of them stood there, and watched Jackie scurry out of sight. When they were sure the kid was out of the line of fire, not that there would be anything violent happening, unless Alden got his hands on Karl or Roscoe.

"All right. We split up. Three go in from this side, and the other three come in from the back. He's less likely to try anything if he's surrounded." Digs met everyone's gaze, but he stopped when he met Alden's. "Once we get your Gypsy, your job is to get Percy free of those fucking silk ties."

"Right."

Alden didn't really want to be involved in whatever punishment the Tramps had come up with for Karl and Roscoe. Tramps might have been seen as the least powerful of all the magical Beasors, but what they lacked in complicated magic they made up for in deviousness. Tramps tended to come up with unique and vicious punishments, if they were crossed or hurt in some way.

Chal nudged Alden in the side, then turned to look at the other Tramps. "I'll flash Alden and Percy back to Beasor, then I'll return to help you with Karl and Roscoe."

"Sounds good."

Digs, Visi, and one of the other Tramps split off to go around the back of the barn. Chal, Alden, and the last one made their way to the front of the barn. Alden fought the urge to pace, or dash into the building. All he wished to do was wrap his arms around Percy, and never let his friend go.

"I'm not sure what you expect me to do. You haven't allowed me to replenish my power. As often as you've claimed to know all about Gypsies, you don't know anything. My magic isn't unlimited, and you've been using me like I won't run out."

Alden froze when he heard Percy. He ached at the sound of his familiar voice, but his hands clenched at how tired Percy sounded. If Percy was healthy and his magic fully recharged, he'd be slicing the person up with his sharp tongue.

Glancing over at Chal, Alden saw the Tramp shake his head. They had to wait until the rest were in position before they could move. As far as they could tell, Percy wasn't in any real danger at the moment. Alden ground his teeth in frustration.

"Do you really think hitting me is going to make it all suddenly better? I can barely stand. My ass is sore from you and your buddy using me like I was some kind of blow-up doll. You aren't going to win anything at the track today because I can't talk to the horses." Percy paused.

Alden strained to hear what the human was saying, but the man's voice was too low.

As weak as Percy seemed to be, his contempt for his captors rang through in his laughter. "Yes, I did enjoy sex, but not while I'm tied up by two men who have only a passing acquaintance with soap and water. Why don't you let Roscoe tie you up and see how you like it?"

"Let's go."

Chal gave Alden a shove, and Alden ran into the barn. He didn't look around as his gaze zeroed in on Percy, leaning against a wooden rail. Alden trusted that Chal and his friends would keep Karl and Roscoe from hurting him. He paused long enough to pull the blade from his boot before continuing.

"Percy," he called.

Percy's head came up, and his friend's face broke out in a huge grin. All Alden could see was Percy, bruised and battered, waiting for him. There were shouts and the sounds of struggling going on around him, but he didn't care. All that mattered was getting to Percy, and saving him.

He skidded to a halt beside Percy, and grabbed the silken ribbons wrapped around his friend's wrist. Pain rocketed through Alden's body, but he ignored it, because Percy had to have been feeling twice as bad as Alden. Not even the most intelligent Beasors could figure out why silk affected the magical Beasors so badly.

The moment his blade cut the silk off Percy, Alden allowed the ribbons to drop and embraced him, crushing the Gypsy to his chest. Percy buried his face in Alden's chest, and collapsed against him.

"It's all right. I've got you, and we're going home, love. You're safe."

Percy didn't say anything, just gripped Alden tighter. Alden kept murmuring reassurances while he glanced around to see Chal. The Tramp walked up to him and clasped both his and Percy's arms in his hands.

"Here we go," Chal warned.

Alden nodded, not caring as long as Percy was with him when they got home.

Chapter Five

Tingling brought Percy back to himself. Blinking, he tried to remember where he was. The last thing he really remembered was Alden wrapping him in his arms, and telling him he was safe. Was that real, or had it been a dream brought on by wishful thinking?

When his vision cleared, he studied the ceiling above him for a full minute before it struck him that he could see it. The room was bright and sunshine streamed in through open windows. It still wasn't his own room, but it was far better than the hole he'd been held in.

Percy took a deep breath, and slowly started to push himself up. The rustle of clothing caused him to swing his head around.

"Here, let me help you." Alden stood from where he'd been sitting, and started to come over to the bed.

"No. I'm all right. I can do it myself," Percy said quickly, not wanting Alden to touch him.

Alden hesitated before returning to his chair. Percy unclenched his hands and managed to sit up, leaning back against the pillows. He looked around, this time paying attention to things. The room was decorated in neutral beige, and it seemed rather sterile.

"Am I in a hospital?"

"Yes. When Chal flashed us back home, you wouldn't wake up. I called Kiki, and she told me to bring you here. This is supposed to be the best hospital for Gypsies in Catalai." Alden shrugged. "I thought you weren't ever going to open your eyes again."

Percy could hear the worry in Alden's voice. He wanted to reach out to his friend, but his skin crawled at the thought of anyone touching him. Oh, he knew Alden wouldn't hurt him, and he was quite willing to bet none of the nurses or doctors would, either. Yet something in his head screamed at being touched.

Calming his nerves, he held out his hand. He could do this. He could hold Alden's hand because he knew both of them needed the connection. Alden moved the chair closer, and took Percy's hand carefully in his. Every move Alden made seemed thought out and cautious, like Alden sensed Percy was skittish.

"Physically, how are you feeling?"

Percy took stock of his body. Nothing hurt anymore, but his wrists were red, and he winced when he saw the pink scars encircling them.

"The doctors said there wasn't anything they could do to fix those. They did say, once your magic was back to full power, you could probably use it to make them not look so bad." Alden shrugged. "Not sure how that works."

Smiling, Percy nodded. Alden had never really understood how Beasor magic worked. Being a normal Beasor, he'd never had to worry about learning how to control power. Percy had never taken the time to explain to Alden how having power underlined their identity as a Gypsy, Tramp, or Thief.

Percy searched for his magic, but there was an emptiness deep inside. He jerked away from Alden, and placed his hands palm to palm, resting them on his chest. Percy closed his eyes, sinking deeper inside his soul. Meditating, he followed his normal channels to find the place where his magic lived. There was nothing there, not even the slightest hint that he used to have magic living there.

His eyes shot open, and he stared at Alden in pure horror. "It's not there!"

"What's not there?" Alden frowned.

"My magic. It's gone—like it's never been there at all." Percy struggled with the bed sheets, trying to throw them off.

Alden stood, but didn't touch him. "Don't, Percy. I'll call the doctors, and have them come to check you. Maybe they can fix it."

"I want to go. I need to get out of here." Percy fought to get up, but his strength was failing him.

Alden pushed a button before resting the tips of his fingers on Percy's hand. It was a light, gentle touch, which froze Percy where he sat. He looked into Alden's face, and gasped at the tears shining in Alden's eyes.

"Please, wait until the doctors get here to talk to you. Maybe they can help you with this. If not, we'll leave, and find someone who knows how to get your magic back."

Percy took a deep breath, and nodded. He turned his hand over and entwined his fingers with Alden's. As much as his mind didn't want any kind of touch, he didn't want to be left alone when the doctors came in. He didn't want to hear his magic was gone forever.

"Stay with me," he pleaded.

"Of course, Percy, I won't leave you alone until you tell me you don't want me around." Alden glanced over his shoulder, probably checking to see if anyone was coming. He leaned closer to Percy, and whispered, "I love you, Percy, not just as my friend, but as the man I want to spend my life with. I won't leave you ever."

Before Percy could get his brain connected to his tongue, the doctors strolled in. They wanted Alden to leave while they examined Percy, but neither one of them would agree to it. Alden moved to the corner of the room where Percy could see him, but so that he wouldn't interfere with the doctors.

After checking him over, and listening to him explain about not having any magic, the doctors left to talk in the hallway. Alden came back to stand next to the bed. Percy wanted to take hold of Alden's hand again, but he couldn't do it. Now that his panic had eased a little, he couldn't bring himself to touch Alden.

Alden didn't try to intrude, but he stood so close that the heat from his body seeped into Percy's, whose shoulders lowered when he allowed himself to relax. He wasn't alone at the moment. The doctors returned, and Alden placed his hand on the pillow by Percy's head.

"Mr Harlow, we must admit we've never really dealt with an issue like yours. We're led to believe if you just rest your power will come back to you. In addition, there are certain activities you can do to replenish your magic as well."

"Really? What are they?" Alden spoke up, and the doctors turned to look at him.

Percy saw the disdainful looks they gave Alden, and anger surged in him. "Alden is my closest friend. You won't treat him any different than you'll treat me."

The prejudice most magical Beasors had against those who didn't have any power annoyed Percy, which was why he'd chosen to live with Alden instead of staying with his family on their compound. He wasn't going to let anyone treat Alden that way.

"I'm not sure Mr Harlow would appreciate us discussing such personal matters with you, even if you are a close friend."

Alden started to speak up, but, before either of them could say anything, a cool voice came from the doorway.

"I will take over, if there is nothing physically wrong with Mr Harlow."

Percy looked beyond the doctors' shoulders to see a slender black-haired young man standing there, arms crossed over his chest. His gold eyes gleamed with impatience.

"Yes, sir."

Alden and Percy watched in surprise as the doctors scurried from the room. The Thief observed them with narrowed eyes, displeasure practically oozing from every pore. It wasn't until the last doctor had left and they were all alone that Alden burst out laughing.

"Who the hell are you, Steril, that you can run an entire group of doctors out of the room?"

Percy didn't like the surge of jealousy running through him when Alden hugged the smaller man. Alden loved him—he wasn't supposed to be hugging other men. Percy rolled his eyes. It wasn't like Alden was going to bend the man over the nearest chair and fuck him.

Alden wasn't like that. If he said he loved Percy, and nothing would make him go away, then he meant it. Percy would just have to get used to knowing that, but never knowing if he could be what Alden needed. His head started to ache. Now was not the time to worry about his relationship with Alden. He needed to focus on what he had to do to regain his magic. Without it, he was nothing, because no one would want him around without being able to give them something in return.

"Who is this?" Percy winced at the snotty tone of his voice. He didn't want Alden and the Thief to know he was jealous.

"This is Steril. He's a Thief who offered to help look for you when you were missing." Alden dragged the pretty guy over to Percy. "Steril, this is my friend Percy. Well, he's more than my friend. Percy is the most important person in the world to me, and I'm so glad he's home."

Steril flashed a bright smile at Percy, but didn't offer his hand to shake. "I'm glad Chal got my message. I wasn't able to come and see you personally, Alden. They wouldn't let me leave the facility again."

"You were the one who got the information about where Percy was being kept?" Alden stared at Steril.

"Yes." Steril blushed slightly. "I might not be much to look at, but I'm part of one of the most powerful Thief families on Beasor. My name gets me certain respect. Also, when I say I'm looking for something or someone, people tend to take notice. I have some friends in the human universe who heard the rumours of a Gypsy being held captive. Then, when Alden's name was mentioned, I knew it was the right Gypsy."

Percy swallowed his pride, and gave Steril a small smile. "Thank you for doing what you did. I'm not completely sure how you did it, but I'm home with Alden, and that's all that matters right now. Well, that and being able to get out of this hospital."

"You can." Steril gestured to the door. "I talked to the doctors while they were out in the hallway. I'm not sure why they were hassling you, aside from the fact they're a bunch of arrogant assholes. I can take you both back to the bar, and we can talk there about some of the things you can do to replenish your magic quicker."

Alden looked at Percy. "Do you feel up to heading home?"

"Yes. I just need to get some clothes on. I'm not wandering around naked."

"Well, I'm sure people wouldn't mind you strolling through bare-assed." Alden winked at him, but Percy shook his head.

"I'm not going to argue with you. Just see if you can find me some clothes."

"All right." Alden wandered out of the room, in search of some robes or something.

Steril looked at Percy. "I have to say I've never seen anyone so worried about a person as Alden was when he didn't know where you were. I wish I had someone who cared for me like that."

Percy smiled. "Alden's always cared about me, and he's been there for me when no one else was."

"Well, one of the ways you can replenish your magic should be pleasurable for you, then," Steril commented.

"What are you talking about?" Percy sat up and swung his legs over the edge of the bed. He steadied himself, bracing his hands on either side of his thighs. His head whirled and his stomach roiled, but he breathed through his nose and it eased his nausea.

"Since Gypsies are such sexual creatures, one way to replenish your magic is by having sex."

"You're kidding me?"

Steril shook his head. "Nope, but I don't think it'll be a hardship for you, right? I mean, don't get angry or anything, but Alden is hot, and you wouldn't have to force me to sleep with him."

Percy gave a low growl, and Steril's eyes went wide.

"I was just saying, man. I wouldn't have done anything, because have you seen the way Alden looks at you? He doesn't see any of the rest of us." Steril held up his hands.

"I found some actual clothes for you, Percy. I didn't think you'd want to wear a robe home." After walking in, Alden paused, sensing the tension between Steril and Percy. "What did I miss?"

"Nothing. Can you help me get dressed? I'm not sure I have enough strength to do it on my own."

Alden set the clothes on the bed, and stepped closer. "Are you sure?" he whispered, shooting a quick look at Steril. "I know you don't want anyone to touch you right now, and I totally understand why, but I'll need to, if you want to get dressed."

Percy stared into Alden's face, and saw all the worry and caring in it. How had he gone so long without seeing the love in his friend's gaze? Percy closed his eyes, and leant forward, knowing Alden would catch him.

"It's something I'm going to have to deal with, Alden. Please be patient, and I promise I'll be worth the wait."

Alden caressed the back of Percy's head with his fingers, not stroking him too hard. "I've waited for you for years, Percy. A few more won't matter."

"Thank you. I love you, too," Percy admitted. "Will you help me?"

"Of course."

Percy let Alden step back. Steril turned his back, giving Percy some privacy to change. He appreciated the kind gesture, and knew he owed the Thief an apology. Percy didn't understand why he couldn't seem to get his emotions under control. Sure, he'd been rather flighty before, but nothing like this. Usually he could be nice to other people, even if he didn't necessarily like them.

They managed to get Percy dressed without Alden touching him too much. Even the few brushes from Alden's fingers caused Percy's skin to crawl. He flinched when Alden's hand landed on his back.

"Sorry," Alden murmured, tugging Percy's shirt on quickly before stepping away from him.

"No, I'm sorry, Alden. It's just they weren't nice to me when I was held captive. I can't just forget about it the moment I'm back home," Percy snarled at Alden, and all the while he yelled at himself silently to shut the hell up.

Alden clenched his jaw, but, before he said anything, Steril turned to look at Percy.

"None of us thought you'd be the same. No one would be after what you went through," Steril commented.

"Let's go." Percy stood, and weaved.

Alden stayed close by, but he didn't try to help or even speak to Percy. Was he angry or hurt because of what Percy had said? Was he being understanding and trying not to crowd him? Percy didn't know, and his head ached with all the thoughts racing through it.

Steril led the way while Percy followed, and Alden brought up the rear. Percy twitched each time someone came near them, though he realised they weren't going to grab him. In Beasor, no one would touch a Gypsy—or any magical Beasor. The consequences could be dire for anyone who did so. Also, Alden would keep Percy safe, no matter what.

The way everyone avoided them told him Steril might be far more important than they had thought. No one would meet their gaze, and Steril strolled through the building like he owned it.

Alden moved closer, but not enough to invade Percy's personal space. "Something tells me Steril's family might be even higher up on the Council than we think."

Percy nodded his agreement with Alden's whispered comment. They continued out of the hospital, and over to a hover sled idling at the kerb. The door slid open when they approached, and Steril stepped to one side, motioning for Percy and Alden to climb in.

After they'd settled in the seat, Steril leaned in. "I'll send you home. I have to do some business downtown, so just shut the door when you're done, and the sled will come back to wherever I am."

"Thank you, Steril. We owe you." Alden clasped Steril's arm.

The Thief smiled. "I'll keep that in mind. Never know when I might need a favour."

"We'll help you out, if you need us," Percy promised.

"Be safe, and don't do too much. Also, I'll send you more information on how to replenish your magic quicker, Percy." Steril winked at him before moving away and shutting the door.

"Wait. Wasn't he supposed to talk to you about something you can do to build your power back?" Alden reached for the door.

"Don't worry. He told me while you were getting me clothes." Percy shrugged. "I'm not sure it'll work for me. I might wait to see if just resting will help bring my magic back."

Alden settled into the corner of the seat with his back to the door. "Was it something so terrible or weird you don't think you can do it?"

Percy bit his lip. He didn't want to tell Alden what Steril had said, because he knew Alden wouldn't have a problem with doing it, but Percy worried about his mind shutting down. What if he completely shut Alden out when they started to make love? How much would that hurt Alden? One thing Percy never wanted to do was hurt Alden.

"I don't think I'm up to doing it right now. Maybe, if I don't get better with rest, I'll consider it. Don't worry about it since it's not anything dangerous. When I'm ready, I'll tell you."

Alden nodded, seeming willing to accept Percy's explanation. Silence filled the sled as they rode to the pub. Percy fidgeted, picking at a small hole in the leg of his pants. He wanted to throw himself into Alden's arms, beg for him to hold him, and lose his mind while his best friend and only love kept him safe.

Yet, every time he moved in Alden's direction, some voice inside his head yelled not to do it. While his heart knew Alden wouldn't hurt him ever, his mind told him no one could be trusted. Percy stared at the floor, wishing they were already at the bar. He wanted to lie down and sleep some more. Maybe his magic would start working again.

The sled stopped in front of the bar, and they climbed out. After shutting the door, the sled raced off while they stared at the entrance. Percy heard the voices inside, and he trembled. Alden brushed his fingers over Percy's hand.

"Why don't we go around to the side? You can see everyone tomorrow morning," Alden suggested.

Percy nodded, simply allowing Alden to lead the way. They headed up the outside set of stairs, then entered the apartment. After shutting and locking the door behind them, Alden turned to look at him.

"Do you want to take a shower before you go to lie down?"

Percy thought about it before shaking his head. "No. I really just want to lie down right now. I'll take a shower when I wake up."

"Okay." Alden didn't say anything else until Percy reached the door of his bedroom. "I'm glad you're home, Percy. I know you have things to work through, and I'll wait for as long as you need me to, because I love you, and my life wouldn't have been the same without you."

Percy stared at the door in front of him, and nodded. He went in, stripped, and climbed into his bed. He pulled the blankets up over his head, and closed his eyes. He let all his worries and tension drain from him.

He was home, and safe. He'd do what he had to do to get his magic back, and maybe someday he'd be able to make love to Alden without freaking out. But he didn't have to solve the problem right then. Sleeping would be the best thing for him.

* * * *

Alden stared at Percy's closed door, and sighed. Percy was home, and Alden was so excited he was back, yet something was wrong. He bumped the back of his head against the door. Of course, something was wrong. Percy had been held captive, used and abused in so many ways. It was going to take more than one day for Percy to heal.

He pushed away from the door, and shuffled down the hallway to the kitchen. He hadn't had anything to eat since before they'd left to find Percy. After turning on the light, he opened the refrigerator and studied the contents. There wasn't much in there. He had planned on shopping for food during the day, but instead he'd gone looking for Percy.

Having closed the refrigerator, he stood in front of it and rested his forehead against the cool surface. What did he feel like eating? Or did he want to go to bed and think about food in the morning?

His phone rang, and he snatched it from the counter. "Yes?"

"Hey, boss, I saw you head upstairs. Were you hungry? You order it, and I'll send one of the guys out for it." Reagan's voice roared over the line.

Alden thought for a second before he said, "Sure, Reagan. I'd appreciate it. I'm going to order some food from the deli across the street. Send someone over there in about twenty minutes."

"Okay, boss. How's Percy doing?" Reagan sounded concerned.

It warmed Alden to know his employees cared about Percy as much as Alden did.

"Thanks for asking, Reagan. He's doing all right. His physical wounds are okay, and will heal without too much worry."

Reagan grunted. "Guess it'll take time for the memories to fade. They won't go away, though."

Alden's head bouncer sounded like he spoke from experience. Alden frowned, trying to remember what he knew about Reagan. It wasn't much, but Alden hadn't needed to know all of the man's past, since Reagan had been the most qualified for the position.

"Tell Percy, if he ever wants to talk, I'm around to listen. I was in a situation close to his, so I sort of understand where he's at in his mind."

"I will, and, if you need me, I'll be up here, napping. I didn't think travelling between universes was tiring for a normal Beasor like me." Alden yawned.

Reagan chuckled. "It might not drain you like a magical Beasor, but it's still tiring. Especially with you worrying about Percy. Crash for the rest of the night, boss. We got it covered down here."

Alden thanked Reagan again before hanging up. He called the deli, and ordered. After he did that, he went to his bedroom and changed into a pair of loose lounge pants and nothing else. He opened Percy's door and peered in to check on him. All he saw was the top of Percy's blond head peeking out from under the blankets.

Satisfied his friend was all right at the moment, he shut the door and went to collapse on the couch. He couldn't sleep yet with the food coming in a little while. Alden closed his eyes, though, and let his muscles relax. He was home, and Percy was asleep in his own bed. The only thing better would be if Percy was curled up in Alden's bed, but that would come, eventually.

Percy's aversion to being touched would take time to overcome. Alden planned on doing just that, though. Percy was a sensual being, needing touch and loving to be completely happy. Alden understood that, and would begin to help Percy heal that way tomorrow.

He wouldn't force the issue, but he wouldn't treat Percy like he was broken, either. Doing that wouldn't be helpful to Percy. Alden would also go and talk to Steril. He wanted to know what Steril had told Percy would help replenish his magic without waiting.

Alden meant what he'd said when he'd told Percy he'd wait forever for Percy to be ready to love him, but that didn't mean he wouldn't try to see if he couldn't solve Percy's problems a little quicker.

Chapter Six

Alden dodged the glass flung at him, and he cringed as it shattered against the wall behind him. He propped his hips on the counter while studying Percy.

"If you keep it up, I'm going to have to buy a whole new set of glasses," he pointed out.

"Shut up. I don't need your smug face hanging around here," Percy snarled at him.

Alden raised his eyebrow at Percy. "My smug face? Exactly what do I have to be smug about? The man I love can't sleep, has no magic, and doesn't want me to touch him. My apartment is starting to look like a war zone because said man I love seems to be having a breakdown."

Percy wanted to scream at Alden, and tell Alden he loved him, but he couldn't seem to get out of this depressing spiral he was caught in. His magic hadn't returned. Percy had gone to the doctors again. He'd even talked to the quack Kiki had told him about, but nothing had worked. Steril still insisted that having sex with Alden would break whatever wall had been built around his magic. Yet, like Alden had pointed out, Percy couldn't let Alden touch him.

That wasn't to say that Alden didn't put his hands on Percy. There were gentle strokes of fingers over hands, and brushes of hands over arms. Alden would lean against him, bringing their shoulders together every chance he got, but Percy still couldn't let it go any further than that.

He turned away, not wanting to look at Alden anymore. "I think I'm going to move back to the family compound."

"What?" Alden sounded shocked.

"I've decided to move back home. I'm causing you problems, Alden, and I don't want to do that."

Alden ignored Percy's 'no touching' rule, and grabbed Percy's shoulder. Percy didn't flinch, having got used to Alden again, but he did duck slightly.

"Turn and look at me, Percy. Don't use me as an excuse to give up."

Percy whirled, and advanced on Alden. "My magic isn't coming back, and a Gypsy without magic is broken. I'm worthless. Why would you want me around?"

Alden caught Percy's hand as Percy gestured wildly. "I was never your friend because you're a Gypsy. I didn't fall in love with you because of your magic. I love you because you're my best friend, and you mean everything to me."

As much as Percy wanted to believe Alden felt that way, he couldn't bring himself to trust those words. Deep inside, Percy knew Alden told the truth, but the part of his mind controlling his actions screamed that Alden was lying.

No Beasor wanted a broken Gypsy who had been used as a human plaything. Besides, a Gypsy who had lost his magic could be a dangerous creature. Hanging around Alden, or any of their friends, might be a mistake.

"It's been two weeks since you came home, Percy. Have you tried doing whatever it was Steril suggested? Have you even talked to Steril since the day at the hospital?"

Of course, he hadn't tried Steril's suggestion. At one time, having sex with Alden was all Percy could think of and wish for, but now he couldn't even think about having sex with anyone, much less Alden.

"I can't do what Steril suggested. It wouldn't work." Percy jerked away from Alden. "My father says he might have someone who can help, but I have to return to the fold."

Alden took a deep breath, and Percy waited to hear Alden berate him about choosing to go home to his obnoxious family, rather than staying with him. Percy wouldn't blame Alden for being angry with him, yet not even Alden's anger could convince Percy to change his mind.

Suddenly, Alden's warmth left him, and Percy looked over his shoulder to see Alden sitting on the couch. Alden hunched his body forward, wrapped his arms around his waist, and sighed.

"If it's what you want, Percy, I'm not going to stop you from leaving. I guess knowing I love you isn't enough for you to stay and try to work things out here."

The defeat in Alden's voice broke Percy's heart, but he still couldn't break through the doubts and fears weighing him down to do something about it.

"When are you leaving?"

"I planned on going tonight, while you were gone."

"So you weren't even going to tell me? Just let me come home to an empty place?" Alden didn't look at him, just kept staring at the floor.

"I'm sorry, Alden. I really am. I do love you, but I'm not getting past this," Percy admitted.

"And leaving me will help you in some way? Am I holding you back that much?" Alden finally looked up at him. The pain in Alden's eyes almost drove Percy to his knees. "It doesn't matter. I have to go. I hope your father can find someone to fix you, Percy, since it's obvious your magic is more important than my love."

Percy watched Alden stand, and walk out of the apartment. He wanted to beg Alden to stop, but how could he? He was the one who had made the decision to leave. Alden would have stayed with him for however long it took to get his magic back. Yet Percy couldn't tell Alden what was going to happen if his magic never came back.

He didn't want Alden to watch as he slowly slid into insanity. Percy could feel it starting. He hadn't slept for several nights, lying in the dark and watching the shadows morph into monsters or into images of the humans who had held him captive. Voices called to him on the breeze, yet he couldn't tell what they were saying. When he looked, no one was there.

Percy scratched at his skin. It was beginning to itch and burn, like something was crawling underneath it. There had been times when Percy had sworn he'd seen something moving under his skin, but when he'd asked Alden or one of the others to look, they'd never seen anything. Finally he'd stopped asking, not wanting them to look at him with pity in their eyes.

Knocking drew him away from his inner fears. He opened the apartment door to find Chal and Kiki standing there. Percy blinked, wondering if his mind had gone over the edge, because those two together was a vision he'd never thought he'd see.

"Are you ready?" Kiki breezed in, brushing a quick kiss over his cheek.

"Alden told me you might need some help carrying stuff," Chal explained his presence, not moving from the doorway.

"Umm...thanks. Yes, Kiki, I'm ready to go." Percy pointed to several bags. "I'm just bringing my clothes."

"You're not taking your other stuff?" Chal asked while he bent to pick up two of Percy's duffels.

"No." Percy chuckled softly. "Maybe I'm hoping Alden will forgive me, and, when I get my magic back, he'll let me return."

Chal shook his head. "Man, I think you're stupid for leaving in the first place, but I doubt very much Alden would ever tell you no."

"Considering how he wouldn't look at me when he left just now, I'm thinking you might be wrong about that."

He swallowed back his own sorrow. How long had he wanted to speak aloud of his love for Alden? Wouldn't it figure something like this would happen to keep them apart? If he believed, he would think he was cursed, or that God didn't like him.

"You hurt him, Percy. What did you expect he'd do? Be happy you're leaving him?" Chal shook his head. "You're lucky he didn't pitch a fit, and lock you in your room until you came to your senses."

"Oh, what's the big deal?" Kiki whirled around to eye both of them. "Why would you want to live here, Percy? This place is so depressing."

"It's perfect, and I don't want to hear you say anything against it, Kiki," Percy told his sister.

"If it's so perfect, why are you moving back home? Is it because Father said you had to, or else he wouldn't send for the doctor who might fix you?" Kiki shook her head, blonde curls bouncing, as she frowned.

Percy ground his teeth, but nodded. "It's one of the reasons why. I don't want to torture Alden with wanting me, but me not being able to do anything about our desires."

Kiki reached out and grabbed a hold of Percy's hand. Tensing, he resisted the urge to yank away from her. She didn't understand his problems, because he'd never told any of his family what had happened to him. Percy'd only told his father about not getting his magic back. He figured his father would have some way of fixing the problem without having to resort to sex.

As much as he wanted to have sex with Alden, he didn't want to use him to get his magic back. Percy used to imagine what it would be like to be skin to skin with Alden, to sleep all night in Alden's arms, but he couldn't help thinking that any chance he had was gone now.

Chal grunted, and walked out of the apartment. "You're an idiot, Percy, but hopefully you'll get your magic back doing it this way."

"Thank you, Chal."

Before Percy could follow the Tramp, Kiki pulled him to a stop. His sister met his gaze, and he saw something in her lavender eyes that he'd never thought he'd see. Concern and caring shone in them.

"Don't go home, Percy. Come to my place. I have enough room, but don't trust Father. You know he'll do whatever he must to keep you from leaving again. He hates the fact you got free, and your freedom encouraged the rest of us to leave as well." Kiki grimaced. "You know Father wants to be the head of the most powerful Gypsy family on Beasor. He'll get his claws into you, and never let you go again."

"But, if I don't go back there, he won't give me the name of the doctor who can help me. I can't keep living like this, Kiki. I think I'm going crazy, and I'm scared I can't stop it."

Kiki hugged him, and Percy stiffened. His family hadn't been a hugging family to begin with, and not liking to be touched made it worse for Percy.

"You're not going to go crazy, though it's a possibility if you stay at the compound. I mean it, you're going to come home with me, and I'll see about getting the name from Father."

Percy didn't have the energy to argue with his sister. He simply wanted to go somewhere and rest at the moment. "All right, Kiki. I'm not going to fight with you about it."

"Good."

She tried to drag Percy out of the apartment, but he hesitated, taking a moment to look around. He wanted to come back soon, and he hoped Alden would welcome him with open arms, or would at least forgive him. He fingered his key in his pocket, but kept it instead of laying it out for Alden. Percy would use it as a talisman to give him an incentive to heal and come back to the only home he'd ever had.

Percy followed his sister down the stairs to the street, where her sled hovered at the kerb. Chal stood next to the vehicle, his hands resting on his hips, and Percy couldn't meet the Tramp's gaze.

"Keep an eye on him for me, Chal?" Percy asked.

Chal heaved an annoyed sigh, but he clapped his hand on Percy's shoulder. "I'll do my best, but you better get your ass back here. I'm not looking forward to dealing with Alden while you're gone."

Percy shook Chal's hand off his shoulder before climbing into the sled besides Kiki. He didn't look back, knowing there was a very real possibility he'd change his mind if he saw Alden standing, watching him leave.

After the sled had turned the corner, he sat back against the seat, and covered his face with his hands. Percy bit back a sob. God, he was stupid to leave Alden, who loved him whether he had magic or not. Alden had never used him for his power, except to ensure there were no mice in the bar.

"You are a fool, Percy."

He peered through his fingers at Kiki. "What are you talking about?"

"You shouldn't leave that dump. Alden loves you. I never saw a man more upset when he realised you were missing. He actually called Father to find out if he'd seen you. Of course, Father never talked to him, so he called me instead."

"Why didn't he tell me this?" Percy dropped his hands to rest in his lap.

Kiki shrugged. "I know it's been two weeks since you were brought back, but have you really talked to anyone about what happened? Or have you been moping in your room, hiding from anyone who might love you?"

"You don't understand what it's like, knowing your magic is gone, and there's nothing you can do to get it back."

Kiki slapped him, and he rubbed the stinging spot on his arm.

"What the hell was that for?"

"You really are an idiot, Percy Harlow. You know very well there is something you can do to bring your magic back. For some reason you're reluctant to do it. Why are you punishing Alden because of your own doubts?"

"I don't want to talk about it with you, Kiki. Not now, and probably never."

"Whatever." She flopped back in her seat, and crossed her arms. "I'll get you the information about the doctor you need, but don't expect me to be happy for you."

"You never told me you liked Alden," Percy pointed out. "In fact, I'm pretty sure you and the rest of the family looked down on him because he's an ordinary Beasor. None of you ever wanted to meet him, or talk to him. I'm surprised he chose to call you when I was gone."

Kiki wrinkled her nose. "Trust me. I was just as surprised as you, but he called, scared to death, and asked for my help. I did what I could, but it wasn't much, because no one really knew where you'd gone. Alden owes me a favour."

Percy winced as she squealed and clapped her hands.

"I know exactly what I'm going to ask him. I want to have a party for my birthday. His bar is the perfect place for it."

Maybe he should warn Alden what Kiki was thinking. Of course, her birthday was another three months away. Hopefully Alden would be talking to him again by then.

"I'm not sure Alden's ready for you and your friends," Percy teased.

Kiki stuck out her tongue, and Percy laughed. As flighty as Kiki was, she was his closest friend besides

Alden, and she'd always been able to make him smile. After reaching out, he touched her hand.

"I'm sorry I left, Kiki. It probably wasn't fun for you once I was gone."

His father was an egomaniac, who believed it was his destiny to head the most powerful Gypsy family on Beasor. It hadn't worked out how he'd wanted it, since Percy had cut off all contact with his family when he'd moved in with Alden. Kiki had followed in his footsteps, finding her own way in Catalai and doing rather well for herself.

"It wasn't, but your leaving gave me the courage to leave as well. It helped that you were doing well on your own."

"I wasn't on my own. I had Alden to help me out. If he hadn't given me a place to live, I might have been on the streets for a while." Percy closed his eyes, and breathed in. "I can't believe I left him."

"I know. What the hell brought that on?"

"Steril told me how I could get my magic back, but my mind won't let me do it." Percy shuddered, even though it wasn't the thought of Alden's touch making him shiver.

"Who's Steril, and what did he tell you?" Kiki's eyes gleamed. "Is he cute? Would he be interested in a hot woman like me?"

Percy snorted. "I don't think Steril would be interested in you, sweetheart. You don't have the right parts."

"Damn." She pouted. "Why is that always the case?"

"Not sure, honey. He told me having sex would help get my magic back."

He covered his ears as Kiki squealed, and he winced when she slapped him hard on the arm.

"I can't believe you're moping around, worried about not getting your magic back, when all you had to do was jump your roommate." Kiki bounced in her seat and clapped her hands. "Why don't we turn around right now, and you go into the bar, grab Alden, and take him upstairs? You can get your magic back, and fuck Alden. Where's the bad in that?"

Percy turned away from Kiki to stare out of the window at the passing scenery. "There are things you don't understand, Kiki. I don't want to get into why I can't do it."

"You can't do it? It's not that you won't do it, but you *can't* do it?" She narrowed her eyes, and tapped her finger against her lips. "Hmm...that's rather interesting."

The sled eased to a stop in front of Kiki's building. The door to the sled lifted up and Percy climbed out, turning to help his sister. The doorman pulled his bags out of the trunk.

"Can you have those brought up to my apartment, George?"

"Yes, ma'am."

Percy handed the man a tip, and the man touched the brim of his hat. They headed up to Kiki's apartment. As they rode the elevator, Percy compared his old home to Kiki's modern apartment.

Alden's pub was in an older part of Catalai, and so everything was a little bit worn down. Percy liked the way the bar and his apartment looked like it had been lived in for a while. Their furniture was used and comfortable. Kiki's apartment building was all glass and steel, so neat and clean it looked like no one lived there.

The elevator shot up to the third floor and opened without giving Percy a chance to think. They strolled along a wide, well-lit hallway to Kiki's door. She pressed her fingers to the pad, and a click sounded as the door swung inward.

"Very nice. No wonder you weren't impressed by my apartment." He shrugged as he followed her inside. "I still like my place better. It's homier."

She tossed her curls over her shoulder, and flopped onto her white couch in the living room. Her shoes flew across the room when she kicked them off, and Percy winced as one hit the wall, leaving a black mark.

"Come sit with me, and we'll worry about everything later," she demanded, waving her hand at him.

"I think I just want to go to sleep, and see if tomorrow will be better," he said.

"Oh, all right. Your room is down that hall on the left. You have your own bathroom. There's food in the refrigerator if you want it, but I'm heading out to hang with some friends. I'll see you in the morning."

"Thanks." He bent down to give her a kiss on the cheek before heading to his room.

His bags had been delivered to his room by the time he had finished in the bathroom. Percy quickly changed into a pair of soft cotton pyjama pants and a loose shirt. He climbed under his blankets, and stared up at the ceiling.

As much as his body wanted to sleep, Percy had the feeling it was going to be a long night for him. Sleep hadn't been a recent visitor. Percy closed his eyes, though, thinking about Alden instead of all his other problems.

His phone beeped in the tone he'd set up for Alden. Percy considered not answering it because he didn't want to hear Alden get on him about leaving. Yet he also wanted to hear Alden's voice once more that night.

Percy snatched his phone off the nightstand and hit the button. "Hello?"

"Hey, Percy. How are you?" Alden's voice was soft, but he must have called from the bar since there was a lot of background noise.

"I'm all right. Is it busy tonight?"

Percy wanted to tell Alden how sorry he was about leaving, but he didn't want Alden disappointed in him.

"Yes. Chal brought a bunch of his friends, and they're a bit rowdy." Alden paused for a moment before continuing, "Are you okay? Safe wherever you are?"

"Yes. What do you mean wherever I am?" He frowned as he stared at the opposite wall.

"Your father called, demanding I tell him where you were. I told him you left earlier, and as far as I know you were on your way to his place." Alden sounded like he shrugged. "Of course, I'm not inclined to tell your father anything anyway. Where did you end up?"

"Kiki's place. She said she'd help me with things. I just couldn't do it. Kiki pointed out that if I went to Father's, I probably wouldn't be able to get free again."

Alden snorted. "She's right. Your father would more than likely lock you up, and not let you out, even when you got your magic back."

"I think Kiki's a little lonely as well, so this might end up being a good thing for both of us. Oh, by the way, she's decided how you can repay her for helping to find me."

"But she didn't get me any information. I owe Steril and Chal for finding you, and Chal's friends for helping me get you away from those bastards who had you," Alden protested.

Percy laughed. "I know, but this is Kiki. You know what she's like."

"I do. What does she want?"

A voice shouted Alden's name in the background.

"I should let you go. Thanks for calling, Alden. I wasn't sure I'd hear from you."

There was silence on the other end for a minute. Was Alden going to reply to his comment?

"I wasn't going to call, because I'm still not happy that you left." Alden sighed. "But I'm not going to force you to stay, Percy. If you needed to leave, then you needed to leave, and I'll be here for you whenever you want to talk."

Percy took a deep breath, and let the tears in his eyes fall. No one was around to see him cry. "I do love you, Alden. I just can't be with you right now. I need to work my issues out, and I don't want to end up hurting you. I'm afraid that'll happen if I stay there."

"I know you love me, and I know you still haven't been able to deal with the things that happened to you while in the human universe, but I'm not sure being away from me is the best thing for you." Alden grunted. "I have to go, Percy. I love you. Never doubt that, but also know this—I'll let you do this for only so long before I come bring you back here."

Warmth infused Percy as he allowed the knowledge of Alden's determination to fill him. "I understand, and I'm hoping you won't have to come and get me."

"Good night, Percy. Try to get some sleep, and I'll call you tomorrow."

Alden hung up, and Percy practically punched the screen of his phone. He let it drop to the bed next to him. Exhaustion swelled through Percy, but he couldn't fall asleep because the darkness filled in the spaces and moved like snakes waiting to strike.

After sitting up, he touched the base of the lamp on the nightstand, and a soft light illuminated a small space around Percy's bed. He settled back on the mattress, letting his eyes close. Percy thought about Alden's voice talking in his ear, and slowly his fears eased enough for him to slip into sleep.

Chapter Seven

Alden looked up when the crowd at the bar went silent. A flash of fair hair caught his attention and his mouth went dry. Had Percy come back on his own? It had been a week since Percy had left, and, while they'd talked on the phone every day, Alden had never pressured his friend to return home.

He tossed his towel on the back counter, and started to come out from behind the bar.

The minute the Gypsy in the door took one step into the packed bar, disappointment surged through Alden. It wasn't Percy, but the familiar way the blonde carried her head told Alden who it was.

He approached her. "How are you, Kiki?"

Her smile was beautiful, and her eyes gleamed with happiness. "I'm wonderful, Alden. I needed to talk to you, so I wonder if we could find some place quiet."

"Is Percy okay? I just talked to him an hour or so ago." Alden flagged Reagan down. "I'm taking a break, and going upstairs. If you need me, give me a call."

"Certainly, boss." Reagan nodded at Kiki before they wandered off.

"Are all your employees gay?" Kiki stuck out her bottom lip.

"No, but Reagan is. Once we're done talking, I'll introduce you to Roger, Reagan's twin. He likes Gypsies."

Kiki perked up at Alden's offer, and followed him without arguing. They made their way upstairs. Alden fought the urge to pick up the clothes littering his apartment. Percy had been the neat one, and Alden had kept the place clean to make Percy happy. Without Percy around, there didn't seem to be any reason to keep the apartment tidy.

"Percy would have an absolute fit if he saw this," Kiki commented as she stepped over a pair of Alden's shoes to shove a pile of clothes off the couch and onto the floor. She sat down, crossing her legs as she turned to look at him.

"Well, Percy isn't here, so I can do pretty much what I want, right?" Alden stood for a second, staring at the mess his living room had become. "Do you want something to drink?"

Kiki shook her head. "I'm not sure you have a clean glass anywhere in here. I'll get something downstairs after you introduce me to Roger."

"Okay." Alden propped his hands on his hips and studied Kiki. "So why are you here, Kiki?"

She drummed her fingers on her thigh as she glanced around. What was she thinking about? Why had Percy's sister shown up at the bar? Alden's heart jumped when he thought about Percy. Maybe there was something wrong with Percy, and Kiki was there to tell him.

"Kiki, just get on with it, all right? I don't have all night, and I'm going to strangle you if you don't say something right now," he ordered her.

Sighing, Kiki flipped her braid over her shoulder, and fidgeted with the wrinkles in her shirt. "Percy wouldn't be happy if he knew I was here. He didn't want to bother you."

"Bother me? I love him, for Pete's sake. Nothing he does is a bother." Alden dropped to the couch next to Kiki, and grabbed her shoulders. "Is Percy all right?"

He shook her slightly. Kiki grinned at him, and her grin was slightly smug.

"Do you know Percy thinks you don't want him anymore?"

"Not want him? I've told him I love him every time we talk, and I let him go when he wanted to leave. I would have made him stay, but I know he didn't want to be forced into staying." He let her go, and turned around to brace his elbows on his knees. He glared at the floor. "It's not my fault he left. Why would he think I don't want him?"

"Because you haven't come to drag him back here. I think he expected you to let him be away for a day or two before you'd come for him." Kiki shrugged. "I'm not completely sure what he's thinking."

"If you think that's what he wants, then I'll do it. I'll come with you right now, and drag his ass back." Alden shot to his feet.

Kiki rested her hand on his arm to keep him from dashing off. "Don't go yet. You need to know some other things."

"What? Tell me what I need to know, Kiki. I don't want Percy to ever believe I don't love, or need him."

She sighed, and entwined her fingers, letting her eyes drop onto her lap. "I got the name of the doctor my father suggested to help Percy get his magic back."

Something in the tone of Kiki's voice warned Alden he wasn't going to like what she had to say. "Tell me, so I can figure out what I need to do to help him."

"Okay. He's fading away, Alden, and I think he's going crazy. Percy sees things, people or objects, all around him. He hears voices, and he tells me he can feel things crawling under his skin." Kiki shuddered and took Alden's hand. "I'm not entirely certain what the doctor has him doing, but it's not working. I know you think I don't like you, or don't think you're good enough for Percy."

Alden snorted. "I know exactly how your entire family feels about my friendship with Percy, and I don't care. I never have, because it isn't about you. It's about Percy, and making him happy. It's always been about Percy."

"I know." Kiki squeezed Alden's hand. "I might have started out that way, but I've changed my mind. Percy hasn't been happy since he moved in with me."

"Well, it hasn't been a picnic for me either. I just don't understand what's wrong with him. Has he said what might be his problem?"

She shook her head. "I can't tell you, but go talk to Steril, and he might be able to explain what's wrong with Percy, and how you can help him."

"Steril?" Alden didn't know exactly what the Thief had to do with fixing Percy's problem.

"Yes, the Thief who helped you locate Percy. I know he told Percy how to get his magic back, and he'll probably tell you, considering how stubborn my brother has been." Kiki's lavender eyes filled with tears. "I like you, Alden, and I know Percy loves you. He needs you, Alden."

"All right." Alden stood, forcing Kiki to let go of him. "I'll go find Steril, and get him to tell me what I need to do to help Percy get his magic back. After that, I'll go find Percy."

"I'll let the doorman at my building know you're coming. He'll give you a key to get into my apartment. Percy will still be there, because he won't leave, and probably doesn't have the strength to go anyway."

Alden helped Kiki up, and they went downstairs. Alden flagged Roger down, and introduced him to Kiki like he promised. The way their eyes lit up when they saw each other told Alden both were happy for the introduction. He let them wander off while he went to Greta.

"I'm going to find Steril, and talk to him. After that, I'm going to bring Percy home."

"It's about damn time." Greta slapped his back and grinned. "I've been wondering how long you'd last before you broke down."

Alden shrugged. "I couldn't force him to stay, Greta. It would've been too much like being held captive by those bastards."

"I know, boss, but he needs you."

He knew that, and that was why he was heading off to find Steril. Hopefully the Thief would be willing to help him out. Alden smiled at Greta before leaving.

Standing outside his bar, he pulled out his phone and hit the screen. Steril's picture popped up, and Alden touched it to dial. He placed it to his ear while flagging down a sled.

"Yes, Alden. How can I help you?" Steril's voice came over the phone.

"I need you to tell me what I have to do to help Percy get his magic back. He's not doing well, and I'm afraid he's going to either die or go crazy from it." Alden climbed into the back of the sled.

Steril inhaled sharply. "I told him what he could do when I picked you up at the hospital. Why hasn't he done it?"

"I don't know." Alden settled into the seat.

"Meet me at this coffee house." Steril gave Alden the address. "I'll explain what you need to do, and what might actually be wrong with Percy."

Alden repeated the address to the auto-driver on the sled. It slid away from the kerb, and Alden rested his head against the seat.

"I'll be there in ten minutes," he told Steril.

"I'll be there."

After hanging up, Alden folded his phone before returning it to his pocket. He wanted to call Percy, and see if he was okay, but he doubted Percy would tell him either way. He closed his eyes, breathing slowly, trying to calm his nerves. It wouldn't do for him to panic, or to be too emotional when he went to see Percy.

"You have arrived at your destination." The auto-driver's electronic voice came over the speakers.

The door swung open, and Alden climbed out to spot Steril standing outside the coffee house. Alden hugged the smaller man before escorting him into the building. Steril waved to the baristas behind the counter, and headed towards a table in the back.

"Hey, Steril, you want the usual?" one of the girls shouted to him.

"Yes," he yelled back.

"What about your friend?"

Alden shook his head. He wasn't interested in coffee or anything else except getting Percy. They sat, but Steril didn't seem inclined to talk until after his drink had arrived. Once the girl was gone, Steril took a sip. Alden sat on his hands to keep from grabbing the Thief and shaking him hard.

"I know you're worried, and you should be. Any Gypsy without his magic will go insane eventually."

Alden told Steril everything Kiki had told him. Steril nodded and took another sip of coffee.

"If Percy's not sleeping, that's another reason why he's having problems. His energy is being depleted, and he needs help." Steril narrowed his gaze at Alden. "I told him one of the ways he could get his magic back. I wonder why he didn't do it."

Alden shrugged. "I don't know. He never told me what it was. All he told me was he wouldn't do it."

Steril nodded. "Hmm…maybe he didn't want to do it because he didn't want you to feel pressured into it."

"What did you tell him?"

"I told him having sex would help replenish his magic quicker than even resting up."

Alden stiffened and gripped the edge of the table. "Having sex would help replenish his magic, and he didn't tell me? I would've had sex with him without being asked."

Steril snorted. "I know that, and more than likely so does Percy. To be honest, I think he can't bring himself to have sex with anyone, much less you. He loves you, Alden, but he was held captive and used like a sex doll by those assholes. Something like that can mess with a person's mind, no matter how much he tells himself it didn't mean anything."

Alden relaxed his hands, and eased back in his chair. "You might be right. I have to believe it doesn't have anything to do with me personally. He hasn't dealt with what happened to him in the human universe."

The Thief drank his coffee and stayed quiet while Alden worked through his thoughts. Percy needed his help, and, besides loving Percy, Alden didn't want his best friend to suffer anymore.

"Why do you think Percy's magic hasn't come back? I mean, even without the sex, he should be getting some of his magic back," Alden said.

Steril drummed his fingers on the table while he stared out across the crowded coffee shop. "I think he's blocked."

Alden frowned, but, before he could say anything, Steril continued.

"If you were to ask him, he might not be able to tell you himself why he was blocked. I think it's because the humans kidnapped him for his magic, and, once it was gone, he didn't want it to come back. Not while he was still with them. If he didn't have magic, they had no reason to keep him."

Alden pursed his lips and nodded. "You might be right."

Steril shook his head with a soft sigh. "I had a friend who was taken in a different universe, not the human one, though. The same thing happened to her, and she blocked her magic afterwards. Unfortunately, I didn't know how to help her, and she died. It was only after her death that I went looking for answers."

"I'm not willing to let Percy die if there's something I can do to fix his magic. There's nothing I can do to change what happened to him, or wipe out those memories. Only time will make those fade away." Alden pushed to his feet. "I'm going to get Percy, bring him back to our apartment, and, if I have to, I'll seduce him to start getting his magic back."

"Good luck. A Beasor without his magic won't last long, especially a Gypsy. I'm sure Percy's worried you won't want him if he doesn't have magic, because most people wouldn't want him. Most ordinary Beasors see us magical ones as exotic, and there's no reason to keep us around if we can't do magic."

Alden frowned. "I told Percy I didn't care if he had magic or not. I've never asked him to use his magic for me, except for keeping mice out of the bar, but it's not like I couldn't have asked some other Gypsy to do it for me. I love Percy because he's Percy, not because he's a Gypsy."

Steril grinned at Alden. "I know that, and deep inside so does Percy, but he's all screwed up because of what happened to him. You'll have to deal with that after you get his magic back."

"Thank you, Steril. Again, if you ever need my help, let me know. I'll do anything you need to pay you back."

Alden leant down and kissed Steril's cheek. The Thief blushed, and motioned for Alden to leave.

"Get out of here."

He shoved his way out of the coffee house, and flagged down another sled. After climbing in, he engaged the auto-driver to take him to Kiki's apartment building. He closed his eyes, and breathed deep, calming his pulse and nerves. It was time for Percy to come home, and Alden wasn't going to take no for an answer. He cleared his mind and just breathed until the sled stopped.

Alden got out, and the doorman greeted him.

"Mr Sparks?" the doorman asked as Alden approached the door.

"Yes. Kiki Harlow said she would be calling you to let me in her apartment."

"Certainly, sir. Ms Kiki said you were here to help her brother. I hope so, because I haven't seen him since he came to live here."

Alden followed the doorman into the building and to the elevator. The doorman slid in a card and pushed the fourteenth floor button. He handed Alden a key.

"Ms Kiki said it was okay to give you a key to her apartment. Here you go, but please return it to me when you leave."

He took it and nodded. "I will. Thank you very much."

The doors shut, and the car shot up towards the fourteenth floor. Alden twirled the key through his fingers, impatient to see Percy and to drag his soon-to-be lover back to their apartment.

The elevator stopped and the doors opened quietly. Alden strolled down the hallway to Kiki's door. He didn't knock, simply unlocked the door and entered. Looking around, he shook his head. It was definitely Kiki's home, decorated in whites, steel, and chrome. It was almost too much for him.

"Alden, what are you doing here?" Percy's voice came from behind him.

"Trying not to throw up," Alden admitted as he turned.

He froze when he saw Percy.

"Oh, Percy, what the hell have you been doing to yourself?"

Percy was pale and so skinny that Alden was sure a stiff wind would blow him over. His beautiful golden hair hung lank around his shoulders. Percy rested his shoulder against the wall, like he needed something to prop him up because he had no energy.

Percy shook his head. "I'm fine, Alden. I'm surprised to see you here."

Alden stalked over to Percy, encircled Percy's waist, and turned to lead him to the living room. They fell onto the couch, but, when Percy tried to scramble out of Alden's embrace, Alden tightened his grip.

"I know you don't want me to touch you, but I'm not letting you go. No more letting you go off on your own. I'm going to stay by your side as long as it takes to heal you physically. I know it's going to take time for the memories to fade, and I'm willing to wait for you as long as it takes."

Percy froze, and turned to look at Alden. His gorgeous lavender eyes, so much like Kiki's and yet so much more lovable, studied Alden like he was some stranger. Alden reached out, cupping Percy's face with both hands, and leant forward to brush a kiss over Percy's lips.

Alden hadn't planned on doing that, but he couldn't hold back the need to kiss Percy. He wanted Percy to know he wasn't going to cringe away from him or turn his back on him. He eased back a few inches, and Percy stared at him.

"Why did you do that?"

"Because I love you, and I wanted to kiss you." Percy tried to duck his head, but Alden wouldn't let him. "Don't look away from me. I don't know everything those bastards did to you, and I don't need to know. Unless you want to tell me. I'll listen to whatever you want to tell me."

Percy shook his head. "How can you tell me that when you don't know what happened to me? I'm not the same person you knew, Alden. I'm broken, and my magic is gone."

"No, your magic isn't gone. Steril thinks you're just blocked. You're scared of what happened to you because of your magic. If you don't have any, no one can take and use you again."

"Do you really believe that?" Percy tilted his head to study Alden. "Do you think that's why I can't feel my magic?"

"It makes sense. Also, he told me what we could do to get your magic back."

Percy blushed, and again he tried to get away from Alden. "I'm not sure I can do that, Alden. It's taken all my strength not to jump out of your arms and curl up in a corner somewhere."

"I get that, Percy, but you're still here right next to me. I think we can do this. I'll take my time, and you can be in control."

"We'll have to leave the lights on," Percy confessed. "I'm afraid of the dark now. Actually, I haven't been sleeping since I came back from the human universe."

Alden snorted. "You're coming home with me, taking a shower while I make you some food to eat. Then we'll see what we can do to get your magic unblocked."

"I can't eat."

Frowning, Alden eyed Percy. "Why can't you eat?"

"The doctor my father sent said fasting helps prepare the channels better for the magic to start flowing again." Percy waved his hand around in vague circles. "There are a lot of things I need to do or not do, and the doctor said, after two weeks of fasting, we'll do a ritual that should bring my magic back."

Alden laughed and shook his head. "You could be dead by then, Percy. No one should fast for that long—I don't think the doctor knows what the hell he's talking about."

"Father swears he's the best doctor in Catalai," Percy protested.

"I'm sure he's the most expensive doctor, but that doesn't mean he's the best. I trust Steril's knowledge more than some quack." Alden surged to his feet, pulling Percy up with him. "Let's go home, Percy."

Percy glanced over his shoulder towards his bedroom. "I should get my clothes."

"We'll come back tomorrow and get your things. I want you back in our home, and everything else will work itself out."

"Okay."

Alden and Percy left Kiki's apartment, Alden locking the door before they took the elevator down to the lobby. The doorman took the key, wished Percy luck, and flagged down a sled for them.

When they arrived back at the bar, Alden took Percy's hand and dragged him around the side of the building. He didn't want to run into any of the employees before Percy was cleaned up. He knew Percy wouldn't appreciate being seen looking less than perfect.

They entered Alden's apartment, and Percy headed directly to the bathroom. Alden went into his bedroom and pulled out a pair of pants and a shirt for Percy to wear after his shower.

"Here are some clothes, Percy. I'm going to make some food for you. Take as long as you want."

Alden touched Percy's shoulder, but his friend didn't turn around. He stepped closer, wrapping his arm around Percy's waist. He pulled Percy to him, and nuzzled Percy's neck. Percy shivered, but Alden didn't think it was because he wanted him to back off.

Shuddering, Percy sobbed, and Alden embraced him, letting Percy know he wasn't walking away.

"Hush now, honey. It'll be okay. Nothing needs to be done until you're ready. Take a shower. You'll feel better when you're clean. We'll eat together, and then we'll talk some more."

He kissed the side of Percy's neck, and took a step back, slowly letting Percy go. His friend turned to look at him, and Alden gasped as he saw the tears flowing down Percy's face.

"It'll be all right, sweetheart. I promise we'll figure this whole thing out." Alden took Percy's hand in his, and pressed Percy's hand to his chest. "Remember, my heart is yours, and always will be. You and I will get through all of this, but we have to do it together. You can't run off anymore. You have to trust me."

"I do trust you. In fact, you're the only one I can trust. If I didn't trust you, I wouldn't even be able to be in the same room with you. I'm just afraid it'll take too long, and you won't want to stay with a crazy person." Percy rested his forehead on Alden's shoulder.

Alden placed his hand on the back of Percy's head, entangling his fingers in Percy's hair. "I probably wouldn't, but you're not going to go crazy. We'll heal all your wounds, and we'll be stronger for it."

Percy's shoulders shook. "I'm not sure I'm strong enough for this."

"Don't worry. I'll be strong enough for both of us, Percy. Someday you'll be the strong one, but let me hold you tonight."

"All right," Percy whispered.

Alden tugged gently on Percy's hair, bringing the man's face up. He met Percy's wet, beautiful eyes and smiled. It didn't matter who moved at that moment.

Their lips met in another kiss, but this time Percy joined in. It was gentle and soft. It was learning how each other tasted, and sealing a friendship, ready to move on to a more intimate relationship.

As much as Alden wanted to take the kiss deeper, and move to the bedroom, he didn't. He broke the kiss, and smiled at Percy's stunned look.

"Take a shower. The food will be ready for you when you're done."

After a quick pat to Percy's butt, Alden left the bathroom with a whistle.

Chapter Eight

Percy turned the water off and stepped out of the shower. He dried off, then got dressed in the clothes Alden had brought him. Alden had been right. He felt a lot better after cleaning up, and his stomach growled as he left the bathroom to head to the kitchen. Pausing just outside the room, he listened to Alden humming quietly to himself as he moved around the kitchen.

A smile crossed Percy's face as he realised how much he had missed Alden's slightly out-of-tune hum. Alden was tone-deaf, but it didn't stop him from singing when he was happy. Some tension eased in Percy when he heard that sound.

He stepped into the kitchen, and Alden glanced up from where he was standing by the stove. Percy didn't stop to think. He just stalked across the room, grabbed Alden, and planted a kiss on his smiling lips. When his lungs begged for air, he broke off, and moved back to the table, where he sat. Alden stayed by the stove, blinking in surprise, until Percy coughed.

"Are you going to sit with me or just stand there gaping at me?"

"Umm...well, I'm not hungry, but I'll sit with you." Alden carried over a plate, setting it in front of Percy before he sat across from him.

"Did I surprise you?" Percy took a bite of his food and moaned. "I'm never fasting again."

Alden snorted. "I'm shocked you lasted as long as you did. You've never been a guy to skip your meals."

"Are you saying I'm fat?" Percy glared at Alden for a second before taking another big bite.

"Man, fat you are not, but you do appreciate food, which makes me happy." Alden touched the back of Percy's hand. "I've missed feeding you."

Percy turned his hand over to entwine their fingers. "I missed having you cook for me. You do realise you completely spoiled me. I found I couldn't do much for myself, and Kiki is worse than me."

"It must have been interesting to have the two of you living together. Does she have someone come in and cook for her? Or clean up after her?"

Shuddering, Percy shook his head. "You have no idea how bad it is. I finally actually hired a maid service to come in. I wasn't eating, so she basically ate out every night."

"Don't look around you, but I haven't done a good job keeping things neat around here while you were gone. I promise I'll pick everything up tomorrow while you rest."

Percy squeezed Alden's hand. "I can't expect you to be perfect. That's what I'm here for."

Alden rolled his eyes, and Percy laughed. He paused, realising it had been the first time he had laughed since moving to Kiki's. He should have known better than to leave and expect his world to work. Nothing in the universes was the same without Alden.

"Why did you leave the first time, Percy? You never told me, and I never asked because I didn't want to bother you about it." Alden ran the fingers of his free hand over Percy's knuckles.

"It was stupid. You were flirting with some guy, and I think you might have leaned over and kissed him as well. I don't know why, but it was like the last straw, and I had to leave. I decided I wanted to go somewhere and think about how I felt about you. I've loved you for a few years now, Alden. I mean love you like a man wants to love a partner, not just as a best friend."

Percy looked down at his plate for a moment before looking back up to meet Alden's gaze.

"It was stupid. I should have just gone to Kiki's, or back up here to think. I don't know why I went all the way to the human universe." He shrugged. "You know me. Impulsive is my middle name. Yet, while I was captive, I vowed I'd tell you how I felt. Too bad it took something like that to make me man up enough to be willing to risk our friendship by telling you how much I loved you."

"Yes. I would've liked you to have come to your senses without being abused like that." Alden nudged his plate. "Keep eating. You need to build your strength up."

Percy did as Alden told him, and finished the rest of the food. He drank the glass of wine Alden had poured for him, after which he stood to take his plate to the sink.

"I'll get that. You go on into my bedroom."

He froze at Alden's words. Percy's heart skipped a beat, and he swallowed before turning to speak, but Alden was there to press a finger to his lips.

"Don't panic. We'll share my bed, and if things happen, things happen. If they don't, they don't. You need to sleep, Percy, and something tells me you might sleep better if I'm in the bed, holding you."

Inhaling deeply, Percy grabbed hold of his courage and nodded. It was Alden, and he wouldn't hurt Percy, no matter what. Percy stood there for a second, mentally slapping himself on the forehead. For three weeks, he'd struggled to fix his problems on his own. Or to ask for help from people who had no real clue how to unblock his magic.

Yet Alden wanted to help Percy. He wanted to fix him, but not if the cure was worse than the issue at hand. Alden loved him, and he'd turned his back on the man. Almost like telling Alden he wasn't important enough in Percy's life for Percy to truly believe he would be able to help.

"All right."

He left the kitchen, and went to the bathroom. After brushing his teeth and changing into sleep pants, he wandered into the other room, climbed into bed and waited. He'd left the light on, and he hoped Alden remembered how Percy felt about the dark.

Alden had gone to the bathroom before he came into the bedroom. He didn't even reach for the light switch, like Percy had been afraid he would have. Percy watched as Alden slid under the blankets, rolling over on his side to allow Alden to spoon him.

"I won't turn off the light until you tell me it's all right," Alden murmured. "I assume they held you in a dark place without any light."

Percy nodded, and bit his lip. He had to talk about it, or he'd never start getting beyond what happened to him. What Alden said was true. His ordeal wasn't something he'd forget about, but it was something that would fade in time, and he would learn to deal with the scars left behind.

"Yes. They tied me to a bed in the dark, and the only time I got out was when they took me to the track. I never saw anything else beyond the track, and being dragged through the house back to my prison. They didn't turn any lights on in the room. I guess they didn't need to actually see anything when they came to screw me."

Alden stroked his hands over Percy's chest, and Percy let Alden's gentle touch ease him. He closed his eyes, and breathed. Alden's familiar scent filled his nostrils, reminding him the man who held him was Alden, his best friend in the entire universes.

Neither one of them had put a shirt on, and Percy shuddered as their skin touched. Alden's lightly furred chest rubbed over Percy's naked back, drawing a sigh from Percy.

"That's it, love. Just feel. Don't think about what's happened before, or what's going to happen in the future. Trust me, and we'll start making things better for you." Alden nibbled along the curve of Percy's neck. "I won't ask you to close your eyes because it'll just make you think you're back with them."

"Even if I did shut them, I'd know I'm not back there. It smells too good. Hell, you smell better than Karl and Roscoe did."

"That's because I know how to use water and soap," Alden teased, as he pinched Percy's nipples.

"Oh," Percy moaned and arched his back, pressing his ass against Alden's groin while gripping the sheets with his hands.

Electricity shot through him while Alden continued to play with his nipples. Alden sucked on Percy's earlobe before easing away from him.

"Wait."

"It's all right. I want you to roll on your back. I need to see your face in case you can't tell me if you're upset or not."

Percy rolled on to his back, and Alden leaned over him. Percy's throat started to close as he remembered being pinned to the mattress with Roscoe or Karl forcing him down. He gasped and grabbed Alden's shoulders.

"Stop."

Alden froze instantly. "Are you okay? Does this remind you of them?"

Nodding, Percy swallowed. He blinked, and loosened his hold on Alden.

"Do you think it would help if you were on top?"

"It's possible."

Percy squeaked as Alden rolled them so that Alden was on bottom and Percy straddled him.

"It's all about you, Percy. You take this as fast or slow as you need to, and I doubt I'll stop you." Alden wiggled his eyebrows and Percy laughed.

Without saying a word, Percy leant down and pressed his lips to Alden's. He licked the seam of Alden's mouth, and Alden allowed him in. Their tongues teased and stroked, learning each other again. Percy ran his tongue over Alden's teeth once before inching away to kiss along the line of Alden's jaw, drawing a shudder from Alden.

Percy worked his way down Alden's neck to suck up a mark on Alden's skin. He bit the muscle of Alden's shoulder, while rocking his groin into Alden's erection. Alden rested his hands on Percy's hips, but didn't grab him or restrict him in any way. It appeared Alden had meant what he'd said about Percy being in charge.

"We need to get naked," Percy said, enjoying the friction of their pants rubbing together, but wanting more skin-to-skin contact.

"Fine by me."

Alden lifted his hips off the bed, and somehow managed to strip his pants off without displacing Percy, who struggled with his own clothing. Soon, their erections grazed each other without any sort of impediment. Percy braced his hands on Alden's chest and rocked, loving the way Alden's cock felt against his.

"Why don't you bring that up here?" Alden suggested, tapping the head of Percy's cock with his finger.

Percy flushed. It had been so long since anyone had pleasured him. Neither of the humans who had held him captive had been interested in making it pleasurable for him. He slowed his movements as his mind began to wander back into those dark moments.

"Oh, no, love." Alden flicked Percy on the nipple. "Keep your mind right here. No wandering away from me."

"Ow!" Percy slapped Alden's fingers away. "Why'd you do that?"

"Got you back to what's important, right? Your cock in my mouth? Like now?"

Percy met Alden's gaze and blinked. "Right."

He slid up Alden's body until his knees were snug against Alden's armpits. He rose up enough to bring the tip of his cock to Alden's lips. Percy groaned as Alden slipped his tongue out, and ran it over the spongy head. He watched Alden point his tongue, and press the tip into Percy's slit.

"God," Percy moaned, his hips twitching with the need to thrust into Alden's mouth.

Alden tipped his head slightly, and met Percy's gaze. "Do you want to fuck my mouth?"

Percy nodded, and Alden grinned.

"Then go ahead. I'm ready for you."

Alden wrapped his lips around Percy's cock while resting his hands on Percy's hips. Percy hesitated, but Alden didn't make any move to force Percy. He got the feeling they would stay there all night like that, and Alden wouldn't do anything more than lie there.

He shuddered when Alden stroked his fingers over the curve of his ass. "I'm not sure I can do this," he admitted.

Alden let Percy slip from his mouth.

"It's all right, Percy. We can keep doing this, and each night we'll get a little further, until you're finally fucking me." Alden smiled up at him, love shining in his eyes. "I have all the time in the world to help you."

Percy's heart filled with love for Alden, and he licked his lips while gathering his courage. He didn't want to go his entire life without ever feeling what it was like to be buried deep in Alden's ass, or to have Alden fucking him.

"Open your mouth," he ordered.

Alden did as he was told, and Percy slowly pushed forward, sliding his cock into Alden's mouth. Percy didn't want to choke Alden, so he stopped when he was halfway in. His soon-to-be lover shook his head a little, and tugged gently on Percy's hips, asking him for more. Bracing his hands on the headboard, Percy thrust again, each time going a little further in until Alden swallowed around him, and Percy cried out.

Suction and the sensation of moist warmth rocketed through Percy as he fucked Alden's mouth. Alden gripped Percy's butt, massaging the flexing muscles with his strong fingers. Percy lost track of time as he rocked, surrounded by all those sexual feelings.

Alden brushed one of his fingertips over Percy's hole, just a light caress, and Percy shivered. He froze, his cock in Alden's mouth, while they stared at each other. Alden placed his finger at Percy's opening again, but didn't move, letting Percy make the decision on what was going to happen next.

Percy went over all the emotions in his soul at that very moment. There wasn't any fear, or anger, because he could see it was Alden with him in their bed. There wasn't any doubt about Alden loving him enough to keep him safe and not hurt him. He pushed back tentatively, and Alden's eyes seemed to smile at him.

Alden let Percy's length slide from his mouth. "Do you want to fuck me or do you want me to do you?"

"I want you to take me first. I need you to erase what they did to me." He grimaced. "I know it won't be that simple, but it'll help me start replacing the nightmares with dreams."

"All right. Can you reach into the nightstand there?" Alden pointed to the little table next to the bed. "There's a bottle of lube in there. We'll need that."

Percy stretched his arm out, and his cock brushed over Alden's chin, leaving a trail of pre-cum and spit on it. After grabbing the lube, he sat back and chuckled at how Alden looked, with swollen lips and evidence of Percy's desire.

"At least you didn't come on my face," Alden joked as he accepted the slick from Percy. "I should ask. Do you want to get yourself ready for me, or do you want me to do it?"

Doing it himself would be another step towards freeing his soul from the prison it was in. After being back for three weeks, he was ready to try and heal the wounds left by his captivity. He understood it would take more than just getting fucked by Alden to fix his mind, but, if he could start getting his magic back, it might help with the rest of it.

"I'll do it myself," he said as he held out his fingers.

"I'm not going to stop you. I think it's going to be damn sexy to watch you stretch your ass."

Percy blushed, but being embarrassed didn't stop him from coating his fingers with the lube, and reaching behind himself. His eyes closed as he pressed his first finger in there, and Alden wiggled a little on the mattress, trying to get a better view of what Percy was doing.

"You're a voyeur, aren't you?" Percy angled his body enough for Alden to see his fingers sliding in and out of his puckered hole.

"Only for you," Alden quickly said.

Percy thought about saying something, but his knuckles dragged over his gland, and he whimpered.

"Here's some more slick. Three fingers should do it." Alden offered Percy more lube.

After coating his fingers again, Percy proceeded to relax the ring of muscles protecting his inner channel. His cock stiffened, and his balls drew tighter to his body as his desire built. It had been a long time since he'd pleasured himself like this, and he'd forgotten how much he enjoyed it.

He gasped as Alden grabbed him and dragged his face down for a deep wet kiss. They duelled with their tongues while Alden slipped one finger into Percy's ass, joining the three fingers Percy already had in there.

"Alden," Percy whispered.

"I know, honey. Just a second. Sit up, okay?"

Percy eased his fingers out, and managed to balance his body over Alden's. The pop of the lube bottle explained what Alden was doing, because he wasn't touching Percy anymore. Alden's hands brushed the insides of Percy's thighs, and Percy jumped.

Alden wrapped his hand around Percy's leg. "Easy. I'm just coating my cock, then you'll settle on me. You'll take your time, and do it as fast or as slow as you want. This is all about you, Percy. I'm just along for the ride."

When Alden finished, they shifted their bodies so Percy was straddling Alden's hips again. Percy braced his hands on Alden's chest, while Alden held his cock in the perfect position.

"Keep your eyes on mine. Remember I love you, and I'd never hurt you."

Percy nodded when he slowly started easing himself onto Alden's shaft. He didn't hesitate, or think of stopping. All he wanted was Alden, as deep inside him as he could get. There wasn't anything in this experience to remind him of his time back in the human universe.

They sighed as Percy's butt rubbed against the nest of curls at the base of Alden's cock. They stared at each other while Percy relaxed and grew used to the length and girth of Alden's dick.

"I can't believe we're doing this," Alden announced, smiling as they absorbed the intimacy of their bodies, together in such a carnal way.

"It's about time," Percy commented, and lifted up until only the head of Alden's cock remained inside. "I'm sorry I was such an idiot, Alden. If I hadn't gotten jealous and flashed to Earth, we might have been fucking before this."

Alden shook his head. "Don't, Percy. All that is behind us. We'll work through your other issues, and get your magic back."

Percy slid back down, and Alden's eyes rolled back in his head. They'd talked enough. It was time to get to the fun part, riding Alden and coming all over him. Alden grabbed his hips and they moved together, one coming down as the other rose up. Their rhythm was perfect, like they were one body and mind.

When Percy thought they needed to go faster, Alden sped up. The sounds of their bodies slapping against each other filled the room, along with their grunts and gasps. Percy was almost there. He could feel his climax hanging on a thread. All it would take was one thrust or touch, but he couldn't prise his hands away from Alden's chest.

"Alden," he whined.

"I've got you." Alden peeled one of his hands away from Percy's waist and wrapped it around Percy's erection.

A couple of pumps and thrusts later, Percy's climax exploded through him, and he shouted as ropes of pearly cum spilled from his cock to decorate Alden's chest and stomach. Alden kept milking Percy until he swore every last drop was squeezed out.

"Hold on, honey," Alden warned, placing his sticky hand back on Percy's hip and planting his feet flat on the bed.

Percy's orgasm made him very malleable to what Alden was doing, and he didn't fight as Alden slammed into him hard and fast. Soon Alden stroked deep inside, and froze, his own seed flooding Percy's passage with hot cum.

When Alden relaxed into the mattress, Percy flopped forward, covering Alden like a blanket. Alden trailed his fingers up and down Percy's back, outlining Percy's spine each time. Closing his eyes, Percy breathed deep and the scents of sex and sweat caused his stomach to tighten.

"Open your eyes, and look around. The lights are on. You can see where you are and who's with you." Alden must have sensed Percy's agitation.

Percy opened his eyes quickly, and rolled off the bed to stand next to it. He glanced around, seeing nothing in the shadows except objects that were supposed to be there.

"Do you need to meditate or something? Isn't that how you gather your magic?" Alden swung his legs off the bed, and put his feet on the floor. He braced his elbows on his knees before looking at Percy. "Maybe we should take a shower before you do whatever you need to do."

They cleaned up, and Alden went back to bed while Percy headed to his old bedroom. Percy put a loose pair of pants on, and sat in the middle of the room. He crossed his legs, and rested his hands palms up on his knees. He closed his eyes, and breathed deeply.

This time, instead of panic and fear, Percy felt calm and peaceful. Maybe it was because his room didn't smell like sex or man. He turned his focus inward, while he continued to breathe softly and rhythmically.

Percy slid along the lines of his magic into the very heart of his soul, where his power pooled to be drawn on when he needed it. His heart skipped a beat when he realised it was still empty. But, before he panicked, he tightened his grip on his emotions and searched the well where it should have been.

While there wasn't any magic there, Percy sensed it wasn't as dark as it had been. Maybe Alden was right about more than just Percy's mind and body needing to heal from the terrible things that had been done to them. Maybe his magic needed to heal as well, and it would take time for it to return, but it wasn't hopeless now.

He'd begun the journey by allowing Alden to make love to him without shutting down or freaking out. It was the first step to fixing what was wrong with him. Percy chuckled softly. A very nice first step, he had to admit, and definitely a step he wanted to keep repeating until he knew every inch of Alden — better than anyone else, better than even Alden did.

Percy stayed seated for thirty minutes, meditating and cleansing his body of all the harsh emotions the day had brought him. Even though it was ending on a high note, and he would never forget it because it was the first time he and Alden had ever made love, Percy knew there were be more bad days than good for a while longer.

A knock sounded on his door as Percy started to stand. Alden peered around the edge with a worried expression on his face.

"Are you okay?"

Smiling, Percy walked up to his lover and kissed him. "Yes, I'm fine. I was just letting all the negative emotions leak away while I tried to remain positive."

"Did it work?"

"What? Remaining positive?" Percy followed Alden back to his room. From now on, he'd be sleeping with Alden, and never alone again.

"Well, that and having sex. Did it help unblock your magic?"

They slid under the blankets and embraced, their legs entwined and Percy's head resting on Alden's shoulder.

"It didn't unblock my magic." He heard Alden take a breath. "But I think it's working. It'll just take more time. I mean, I was gone over two months, Alden. Trauma like that can't heal overnight. I did notice a lessening of the dark, though."

"So what we did helped, at least a little." Alden sounded thrilled.

"It did, and I really do believe, if we keep doing it, eventually my magic will come back."

Alden snorted. "Do you really think I'm going to say no to having sex with you? Never going to happen, my love."

Percy pressed a kiss to Alden's chest. "Good, because I've become very attached to you, and I don't think anyone else would be able to help me solve my problems."

He snuggled closer to Alden, and closed his eyes. This time there wasn't any scent of sweat or sex. It was pure Alden, crisp and fresh with a hint of spice. Maybe he'd be able to sleep through the night in Alden's arms.

Chapter Nine

Percy woke up when a crash sounded somewhere in the apartment. His heart pounded as he lay under the blankets, staring up at the ceiling. Where was he? It was far lighter in this room, and he could actually see the ceiling instead of just shadows. He took a deep breath, enjoying the clean brisk air filling his lungs.

Obviously he wasn't on Earth anymore. Percy blinked as he remembered he hadn't been there for three weeks already. He turned his head, noticing the clothes strewn across the floor, and he smiled when he recognised the picture hanging opposite the bed.

It was a picture of Alden and him at one of their friends' parties. Alden had his arm encircling Percy's waist, and Percy leaned into him. Percy must have been talking to someone out of the shot, because his mouth was open.

Percy frowned as he studied the picture. He climbed out of bed, and padded over to stand in front of it. He wound his arms around his waist while staring at it, and it wasn't the image of him drawing his attention. It was the expression on Alden's face as his best friend looked at him. There was love in Alden's eyes, and a soft smile lifting Alden's lips.

"Why didn't I see it before?" he muttered.

"Because I wouldn't let you, and you weren't ready to see it."

Alden's voice caused Percy to jump, before whirling to look at Alden, who stood with his shoulder propped against the doorframe. Percy tilted his head, and whistled. Alden wore a loose pair of lounge pants, barely hanging on his hips. A few dark curls peeked above Alden's waistband at his groin.

The apartment was warm, so Alden didn't wear a shirt. His chest was broad and lightly furred, which Percy loved since his own chest was smooth. Dark copper nipples were perfectly placed on Alden's pectoral muscles, tempting Percy to pinch or lick them. He really wasn't sure which he wanted to do.

Alden's skin was tanned and his muscles proved he worked for a living instead of sitting behind a desk. *Must be from lifting all those boxes full of liquor bottles,* Percy thought, as he strolled closer to Alden.

He reached out and trailed his fingers over Alden's chest, down to his belly button, where he swirled his finger.

"Hey, stop that." Alden chuckled while slapping Percy's hand away. "You know I'm ticklish."

Leaning closer, Percy buried his nose in Alden's throat and sniffed. "God, you smell so good."

Alden pushed him a few inches away. "I smell like food and sweat. I finished working out before I started making breakfast for us. I don't smell good at all."

"To me, you smell marvellous. The humans who held me hardly ever washed, and they stank to high heaven. I thanked God I didn't have any food in my stomach whenever they came near me, because I wanted to throw up." Percy returned his nose to where it had been, breathing in the nice fresh scent of Alden's sweat.

"I'm glad you like it. Guess I didn't think you were the kind who appreciated the honest smell." Alden tipped his head, giving Percy more access.

Percy rested his hands on Alden's hips, and licked a line along Alden's neck to his earlobe. He sucked on it while Alden moaned. Percy slipped his fingers into the waistband of Alden's pants and pushed them down, until they pooled at Alden's feet.

He dropped to his knees, and eyed Alden's erection. Percy licked his lips before leaning forward to wrap them around the head of Alden's cock. He applied some suction to the spongy glans, and swirled spit around it. After pressing the tip of his tongue into Alden's slit, Percy fisted the rest of Alden's length.

Alden cradled Percy's head in his hands, and arched his hips to slide some more into Percy's mouth. Instead of tensing, Percy relaxed his throat, taking in as much as Alden would give him. He loved the feel of Alden's cock on his tongue and how it filled his mouth.

"Oh, honey. God, I love your mouth."

Percy gripped Alden's hips, urging him to fuck his face. He added more suction and a little scrape of teeth to drive Alden higher. While he sucked on Alden's prick like it was his favourite Popsicle, Percy reached around to run his finger down Alden's crease, and pressed against Alden's opening.

"Go ahead." Alden pushed back onto his finger and winced as it breached his ring.

Soon Alden rocked between Percy's mouth and his finger. Percy closed his eyes, and let Alden take his mouth as fast and hard as he wanted. He didn't care that his jaw would probably ache by the time Alden came.

"Oh, Percy, I'm going to come."

Percy played with Alden, pressing two fingers in and stretching him. He managed to nail his gland, and Alden cried out, flooding Percy's mouth with his cum. Alden trembled while Percy sucked every drop out of him.

"Oh, my God." Alden shuddered as his climax faded away.

After licking Alden clean, Percy rocked back on his heels and caught Alden as his lover slid down the wall to join him on the floor. They wrapped their arms around each other and rolled over, Percy on top.

"Why don't you fuck me, Percy? Take care of this." Alden palmed Percy's erection.

"We need lube."

Percy jumped to his feet, heading for the nightstand while Alden stood and made his way to the bed. Alden stripped his pants from around his ankles, and Percy hadn't got dressed yet, so he didn't need to worry about any clothes getting in the way. He climbed onto the mattress, settling between Alden's spread legs.

He popped open the bottle as Alden slid his hands behind his knees and drew his legs up to his chest, exposing his hole. Percy squirted lube on his fingers, rubbing them together while he tossed the bottle onto the bed. He caressed Alden's puckered opening in warning, before he slid two fingers in.

Alden gasped, but breathed and relaxed as Percy pushed in as far as he could. Percy spent a few minutes continuing to stretch Alden. It was only when he couldn't take it anymore that he stopped. He wanted inside Alden as soon as he could, or else he'd come all over his lover.

He removed his fingers and wiped them on the sheet. After snatching up the lube again, he poured some into his palm, and threw the bottle on the floor. He coated his cock with the slick, and positioned the head at Alden's opening.

"Go on. Take me, love," Alden demanded.

Percy thrust in, not stopping until he was all the way inside. They cried out in unison, and Alden let go of his legs to reach down and grip Percy's ass. Together they rocked and undulated, Percy slamming in as Alden rose up to meet him.

"Damn, I'm going to come again," Alden warned him, and Percy grinned, moving faster and harder to drive Alden over the edge.

Alden's second climax wasn't as powerful as the first, but still his inner muscles clamped down on Percy's cock, milking him until he finally succumbed. He pressed in as deep as he could and stilled, spilling his cum and claiming Alden at the most intimate level.

When his muscles gave out, he collapsed to the side, and they moaned as his softened cock slid out of Alden. He rested his hand on Alden's chest, feeling his pulse slow down until Alden took a deep breath and climbed off the bed.

Percy watched as Alden walked to the bathroom. He closed his eyes, listening to the water run in the sink and the splashes. Alden must have been washing up. Percy knew he should do the same, but he just couldn't gather the strength to do it at that moment.

He rolled on to his back, and flung his arm over his face to try to keep the sunlight out of his eyes. The splat of a wet cloth on his stomach shot him upright in the bed. Percy glared at Alden, who stood in the middle of the room, tugging on another pair of loose pants.

"I'm going back to make some more breakfast. The stuff I made earlier will be cold by now. When you get around to moving, strip the bed and put the sheets in the washer for me."

Alden winked at Percy as he walked out of the room. Percy rolled his eyes, but did as Alden said. He cleaned up, and grabbed the sheets from the bed. He took them to the laundry room and stuffed them in the washer. He even got it started, which took a few minutes, since he'd never done laundry before.

Percy wandered out into the kitchen area just as Alden set two plates on the table. The food looked great, and Percy realised he was starving. He grinned to himself. Maybe the sex was good for something.

"Sit. I'll get you a glass of juice, then you're going to meet up with Steril. You're going to talk to him some more about getting your magic back, and if there's anything else, besides the sex, we should be doing."

"But I like the sex." Percy leered at Alden.

Alden shook his head, and joined Percy at the table. "You always like the sex. Now eat. You're still way too skinny to be healthy."

Percy took a bite and chewed while he thought. After he'd swallowed, he said, "You know, before I got caught, I did like the sex, and I had a lot of partners, even though there was only one I really wanted."

"I know." Alden reached across the table and patted Percy's hand. "We both screwed up by not saying anything sooner."

"True, but I don't think I'd like the sex anymore, if it's not with you. There's something about you that wipes all those bad memories clean. Maybe you do have some kind of magic you didn't know about."

Alden shook his head. "The only magic I have is all the love for you that's in my heart, Percy. I don't have anything remotely close to what you, Chal and Steril have."

"Don't be upset about that. Having the power isn't all it's cracked up to be. Trust me, I've never really seen it as a gift." Percy braced his elbows on the table and propped his chin on his hands. "Maybe it's because I've always been told I wasn't anywhere near as good as my father, or my siblings."

Alden poked Percy with his fork. "It doesn't matter how good you are. Your father is bitter because you and Kiki are making a living without needing his influence to get jobs."

A phone rang, and Alden grimaced as he stretched out to pick it up off the counter. He flipped the screen up.

"Yes?"

"I want to talk to Percy, Mr Sparks."

Percy winced as his father's voice slithered over the phone. God, could his father sound any more oily? Alden turned the screen away, and looked at Percy, who shrugged, and held out his hand to take the video phone from Alden.

"What do you want, Father?"

It was difficult to make lavender eyes look cold and hard, but somehow Percy's father managed to do it. Percy straightened his shoulders and fought the urge to bow his head.

"I want to know what you're doing back at that disgraceful apartment with that bartender."

His father's disdain dripped from the word 'bartender' like it was lower than scum at the bottom of a pond.

"Father, you know full well Alden owns the bar, and I must say it's pretty impressive because he earned the money to buy it, instead of having his father give him the money. I respect a self-made man more than a silver spoon kind of man any day."

If he hadn't been watching his father closely, Percy would never have seen the slight tic in the man's jaw. The jab had landed, and Percy smiled smugly. His grandfather had been a self-made millionaire, earning money working as an animal trainer. He'd become the most sought-after trainer on Beasor, but Percy's father liked to forget the part where his father had worked with his hands. Constantine Harlow preferred to pretend that the Harlows had always been rich, without the taint or stink of a trade around them.

"When are you moving back to the compound, Percy? We talked about this a week ago." Constantine chose to ignore the insult Percy had lobbed at him.

"Well, I got a better offer, Father. I'm going to stay here." Percy shot Alden a quick smile.

His lover smiled back while cleaning off the table and rinsing the dishes. Percy watched the flex of Alden's muscles as he bent and twisted to fill the dishwasher.

"Percy, pay attention. Why stay there? I think your time away has affected your brain more than usual. You're sick, son, and you need to be under a doctor's care."

Constantine sounded like he was sincerely worried about Percy, but Percy knew better. His father had something up his sleeve, and he needed Percy to pull it off.

"My personal physician knows exactly how to take care of you, Percy. He's an expert in blocked magic."

Percy laughed. "You do realise I've been under a doctor's care for over a week now, and it hasn't helped anything. In fact, what he told me to do might have made things worse. Funny thing about that, Father. Your doctor visited me last week, and he gave me advice on what to do to bring back my magic. Turns out, his advice didn't work, which is why I'm back here with Alden, and not at Kiki's or the family compound. The friendly advice I was given by a stranger turned out to work better than your doctor's."

Percy leant back in his chair, and folded his arms over his chest. Grinning, he stared at his father.

"Is your magic back? Are you able to work?" Constantine's eagerness warned Percy his father's call hadn't been owing to his fatherly concern over Percy's health.

"Not yet. Why do you want to know?" Percy studied his father. "Did you promise my power to someone without asking me first?"

Constantine shrugged. "He's a very powerful Beasor, and a member of one of the leading families. I can't do what he wants by myself. You're the only Beasor close to my power, so I told him, once you were healthy, we'd help him."

"And how much is he paying you to do this for him?" Percy shook his head. "Even when I'm back to full power, I won't help you, Father. I'm pretty sure whatever he wants is going to go against my personal ethics code."

He stood up.

"Where are you going, Percy? We're not done talking." Constantine scowled at him.

"I'm done talking, Father, and you'll do well to remember I'm not a child anymore. I can do as I choose. Also, I'm not dependent on you for a living, either. The Gypsy Councilman knows better than to listen to you, so you can't tell him not to give me jobs. Goodbye, Father." Percy reached out and shoved the screen closed.

Alden peered in from around the doorway. He'd left the kitchen while Percy talked with his father.

"I take it he doesn't like the fact you're back living with me, and not at the compound where he can control you again."

Percy rubbed his temples and grunted, causing Alden to stroll over and embrace him. Percy rested his head on Alden's shoulder.

"Constantine has never liked me, Percy. He doesn't think I'm good enough to be a part of your family." Alden nuzzled his nose into Percy's hair.

Percy stiffened. "That's utterly idiotic. The Harlows aren't anything special. We just happen to have a lot of money. It's the only thing making us any different from other magical Beasors. I haven't figured out how Father can be the way he is when Grandpa was very down to earth."

"Unfortunately, your grandfather spoilt your father, and Constantine ended up believing he deserved everything he got as a birthright, not from anyone working long hours to give it to him." Alden hugged him closer.

"What about your family, Alden? I don't think we've ever talked about them." Percy pulled back a few inches to look up at Alden.

Alden's face went blank, and his eyes grew bleak. "I don't know who my family is, Percy. I was dropped off at the Catalai Hospital when I was only a few days old. There wasn't a note, or anything with me, to give a clue of who I might have been."

"Oh, I'm sorry, love." Percy cupped Alden's face and brought his head down to kiss him. It was soft and gentle, and Percy tried to pour all of his love into it.

When they eased apart, Alden smiled at him. "Thanks, but there's no reason to feel sorry for me. I can't miss something I never had, right? Also, after seeing how your family act towards each other, I'm kind of happy I don't have parents to order me around."

"Well, you might not have parents, but you do have a family. Everyone who works at the pub, and a lot of your customers, I'm sure, consider themselves your friends. Family isn't just being blood-related. Some of the best families are the ones you make."

Alden rubbed his nose against Percy's for a second, before giving him a quick kiss and stepping away.

"You might be right. I don't have any more time to discuss this with you. I have to meet one of my suppliers and you need to go see Steril. I'll give you the address of the coffee shop you're supposed to meet him at."

Percy gave Alden a narrow-eyed glare. "All right, but we're coming back to this topic again. I just realised we've almost always talked about my problems since we became friends. You've been remarkably closed-mouthed about your past."

They wandered back into their respective bedrooms to get dressed. When they met in the hallway, Percy pointed back at his room.

"I think I'll be moving my stuff into your room later on. Well, once I get my clothes back from Kiki."

Alden gave him a peck on the cheek. "Sounds like a plan."

Percy laughed. He should have known better than try to shock Alden. The man would've had Percy moved into his room weeks ago, if Percy had got his head out of his ass.

"Percy, let's go. We've wasted enough time with that stupid call from your dad," Alden called from the door.

After grabbing his keys and his credit card, Percy followed Alden down the stairs and to the front of the pub. Alden flagged down a hover sled for him. They kissed, and Percy waved as he climbed in. Alden inputted the address of the coffee house, and tossed a phone on Percy's lap.

"In case you need to talk to me, or just want to say hi," Alden said before closing the door and sending the sled on its way.

Percy smiled and tucked the phone in his pocket. He should have known Alden would have got him one. It would make things easier if Percy was ever kidnapped again. Beasor phones worked in other universes as well. No one was entirely sure why or how they worked, but Percy had never cared enough to find out.

He settled back in his seat and closed his eyes, using the silence in the sled to search out his magic again. It still wasn't there yet, but the feeling was getting stronger. Percy was pretty sure that, in the next week or so, his magic would be back completely. Of course, the more sex he and Alden had might speed up the process.

Percy let his mind empty of all the negative things he'd thought about his father, and let only his happiness at being Alden's lover fill him. Joy was the best thing to help heal an injured Beasor. He ran his fingers around his wrists, and the scars that had been so prominent a few days ago were fading. Soon they would be faint lines, though he would always remember what they represented.

"We have arrived at your destination."

After slipping his card in to pay for the ride, Percy climbed out and stretched as he looked around the neighbourhood. The coffee shop was on the corner of two main streets, but in a part of the capital that was only just beginning to see a renaissance.

Percy pushed open the door and breathed deep the scents of freshly brewed coffee and succulent pastry. Even though he'd just eaten, he was definitely going to have a muffin or something. His stomach would be forever angry with him for passing one of their baked goods over.

"Percy!"

He turned when he heard his name called. Steril stood next to a table in the back, waving at him. He waved back, before gesturing towards the counter. Steril smiled in understanding, and nodded.

Percy got his order and wound his way through the crowd, not liking the crush of people in the small area. He'd have preferred to meet somewhere a little less popular, but it wasn't his choice, so he'd go along with it.

After setting his mug and plate down, he flopped into his chair with a huff of annoyance. He glared at Steril.

"Is there a reason why you chose this place? It has to be busier than the waiting room on public welcome High Council days." He took a bite of his muffin, and moaned. After swallowing, he wrinkled his nose at

Steril. "Okay, so maybe you made a good choice in picking this place."

"I know. Their beverages and pastries are so amazingly good. If I ate here every day, I'd probably weigh, like, two hundred pounds or something like that." Steril grinned, his gold eyes shining with joy. "Luckily, they don't let me out of the facility very often, but when I get a chance, I come here."

The Thief could talk, that was for sure. Percy sipped his coffee while Steril chatted about inconsequential things. Finally, when Percy had finished his muffin, and had only his coffee left, he leant back in his chair and looked at Steril.

"Alden told me to come here and talk to you. I'm not sure what I'm supposed to be telling you."

Steril shrugged. "Alden seems to think I'm the expert on your problem, but I'm not, because I've never had it. I just learned everything I could about it because it happened to one of my close friends, and I didn't want to let it happen again to someone else."

Percy nodded. "Well, you're as close as we have to an expert without me going to the High Council Scientists about it, and I don't want to do that."

"Oh no. They'd keep you for months, or years, and Alden would completely lose his mind if you were gone that long." Steril played with his cup on the table for a moment. "What's it like? Having someone love you like that?"

"I'm not entirely sure. I mean, I've always known Alden loved me, but I'd put us in the best friends box. I never thought we'd move outside of it. Thank God we did, though."

"Have you had sex with him yet?" Steril's cheeks turned bright red, and Percy chuckled.

"Yes, we have had sex." He didn't say any more, resisting the urge to tease the Thief.

Steril nodded quickly. "Good. The more often you have it, the sooner your magic will come back. But even if you were to stop today, and never have sex with Alden again, your power will return. You've unblocked the lines your magic travels through, so you'll be fine."

Percy snorted. "Trust me, Steril, the sex isn't going to stop any time soon."

Chapter Ten

Alden finished wiping down the glass in his hand and set it down with the rest of them. He looked over to where Percy sat, chatting with Chal and Steril. Happiness swirled around Alden's chest when Percy blew him a kiss.

It had been a few days since Alden had retrieved Percy from Kiki's apartment, and they'd become more than best friends. They'd had sex several times since then, and, while Percy's magic hadn't returned yet, Percy swore it was getting closer. Not having magic of his own, Alden had to take Percy's word for it.

He poured a glass of the Pillian wine Percy liked, along with a mug of the ale Chal enjoyed. Steril didn't look like he had drunk any of the drink Alden had mixed for him when he arrived. Alden filled a glass with some Beasor juice, and put them all on a tray. He checked to make sure Greta had everything under control before he grabbed the tray, and headed to Percy's table.

"Here you all are. The way you were talking, I figured your throats were probably dry by now." Alden handed out all the drinks.

Steril looked at his, and Alden chuckled.

"You didn't look like you were enjoying the one I made you earlier. I thought maybe juice was more your style."

The Thief's cheeks turned pink, but he nodded. "You're right. I don't really drink."

"You don't have to drink to hang out here." Percy reached out and patted Steril's hand. "We'll like you, even if you don't like liquor."

"Thanks. Not every Beasor is willing to hang out with a Thief." Steril frowned.

Alden pursed his lips. While most magical Beasors would socialise with ordinary Beasors, all of them seemed to have something against Thieves. Of course, having the ability to steal a person's soul tended to make people uneasy, and, while most Thieves weren't that powerful, there wasn't any way of knowing who was. Also, most Thieves didn't have any qualms about stealing things from people.

"Well, something tells me you aren't the usual kind of Thief," Alden commented. "Besides, this bar is neutral, and, even if you were inclined to steal, you wouldn't do it here."

"You wouldn't want to risk hurting your friends," Percy pointed out, leaning back into Alden's personal space.

Alden wrapped his arm around Percy's shoulders and let his lover relax against him.

Steril nodded. "You're right. I like being here and hanging out with you. I wouldn't risk it, but there are a lot of my fellow Thieves who wouldn't think twice about doing it. That's what I hate most about the facility. They're training Thieves, but not teaching us any morals or ethics."

He fidgeted with his glass, and Alden could tell something was bothering Steril. He leant forward, and tapped Steril's hand. When Steril met his gaze, Alden smiled.

"You do know you can talk to any of us, right? If it's magical ethics issues, then you should probably talk to Percy or Chal, since they're in your position. If it's anything else, you can come to me. I meant what I said about owing you for finding Percy for me." Alden tilted his head, and studied Steril. "By the way, how did you do it?"

"Find Percy?"

Alden nodded. "Nothing Chal and I did worked, but you said you'd find him and you did."

Steril bit his bottom lip, and stared at the table for a moment. He took a deep breath and met their questioning gazes.

"I have a lot of friends throughout the universes, and we've formed kind of a network, I guess you'd say. I put the word out about a missing Gypsy, which was all I needed to do. It travelled through the universes, and reached the right person. I might have mentioned Alden was looking for you, Percy. From what I understand, that's why my friend believed the human who told her. He mentioned Alden's name."

Percy nodded. "I wasn't sure the kid would be able to help me, but I decided I didn't have anything to lose by telling him to ask for Alden. He came through for me, and I wish I could thank him."

"Whatever happened to Jackie, Chal?" Alden shot a glance over at Chal.

The Tramp shrugged. "I haven't talked to Visi since we took care of Karl and Roscoe."

"What did you do to them? Anything painful?"

The hope in Percy's voice might have sounded wrong to most people, but Alden understood why Percy would want his captors to suffer.

Chal's sneer gave a hint to what the Tramps did to the two humans. "You remember the Sublant universe?"

Steril and Percy winced, while Alden had no idea what Chal was talking about. Not being able to flash between universes, he wasn't knowledgeable about which ones were bad or which ones were attractive.

"Yeah. You really took them there?" Percy cringed. "I hated the guys, but I'm not sure, even in my deepest soul, I wanted that to happen to them."

"I didn't pick the universe, Percy. The Gypsy Councilman told us where to take them." Chal shrugged. "I think they got what they deserved."

"What happens in the Sublant universe?" Alden had to ask, even though he thought he might not want to know.

"First, humans don't travel through the universes well. They're not built for it like we are. Second, the Sublants don't like humans at all. If they didn't kill those two outright, they'd play with them for a while. The Sublant universe is mostly inhabited by a humaniod-type feline creature. They like to play with their victims like normal cats do." Chal took a swig of his ale. "I avoid making any runs there, because they're very secretive and dislike any kind of intrusion."

"Yes, the Sublant universe has a 'Do not visit' label for all magical Beasors. A few of the Thieves at the facility have gone there, mostly because it's not allowed." Steril wrinkled his nose in disapproval. "I don't understand the attraction of breaking rules. It never works out well."

Alden snorted softly, and Percy pinched his side.

"Hush. Steril's not like us. He doesn't really seem to have an adventurous bone in his body," Percy whispered.

"Nothing wrong with that," Alden whispered back.

Percy gave Alden a kiss on the cheek, and they all went back to talking about different universes the magical Beasors had visited. Alden didn't feel left out, though he probably should have, but he'd never really wanted to travel the universes. He liked staying on Beasor, and running his pub. All the excitement he might want, he got from loving Percy.

A sudden commotion at the front of the pub caught Alden's attention. He headed over to where Reagan and two of the other bouncers were trying to stop a blonde woman from entering.

"I need to talk to Steril. I was told he'd be here."

"Let her in, Reagan. I'll take her to Steril." Alden gestured for the woman to follow him.

She glared at Reagan, and tugged her clothes back into place. When she turned to meet Alden's gaze, her lavender eyes were blazing. He held up his hand to stop her chewing him out.

"I'm sorry, but Reagan is overly cautious since Percy was taken. Strange, I know, considering it didn't happen here, but there you go." Alden bowed slightly. "If you follow me, I'll take you to Steril."

She allowed Alden to escort her back through the crowd towards the table where Percy and Steril sat. As they approached, the trio glanced up, and Steril's eyes widened when his gaze landed on the woman.

"Xava, what are you doing here? I thought you said you'd never return to Beasor."

Steril shot to his feet, raced around the table, and hugged the woman. Xava embraced him quickly, before stepping back.

"I hadn't planned on coming back, but there's an urgent matter, and I'm afraid I was the only one who could tell you about it. Plus, my mother's dying, and I wanted to clear the air before she was gone."

"If you'd like to have a seat, I'll get you something to drink," Alden offered, pulling a chair out for Xava.

After sitting, she pointed towards Percy's glass. "I'll have the same Pillian he's having."

"Yes, ma'am."

Alden headed to the bar, and poured out a glass of wine. He rushed back, not wanting to miss anything. Silence reigned over the table when he returned. He set her drink in front of her, and reclaimed his seat beside Percy.

"You live in the human universe?" he inquired.

Xava nodded. "Most humans aren't like those scum."

"I was thinking more of how dirty the planet is, and how the humans don't seem to notice or care how they're destroying their home." Alden shuddered while remembering his trip to Earth.

"It takes some getting used to, I'll admit. The hardest thing for me was how much less sunlight there was, even on the clearest, sunniest days there." Xava sipped her wine, and set the glass down before continuing, "I didn't want to stay here any longer, but that isn't important."

"No, you're right, it isn't, and I'm sorry for prying," Alden apologised.

"You needed to talk to me, Xava," Steril spoke up.

She nodded. "You know that kid who gave me the information on Percy here."

Chal grunted. "Sure. Visi and Digs were supposed to help him out after we took care of the other two."

"Maybe that was their plan, but it didn't work out quite like that. He turned out to be missing when they came back to Earth. They looked for him, but, when they couldn't find him, they left word with me and headed out to their next job." Xava ran her finger around the rings on the table.

Alden leant forward and clenched his hands. "Are you saying he's missing? We promised we'd take care of him. That doesn't sound like we helped him. He risked his life to save Percy."

"I know, and the Tramps told me to have my people keep looking. If I got information about where he might be, I was to either get it to them, or tell Steril." Xava looked up at Alden. "I was on Beasor, so it was easier to find Steril, than try to get a message to him."

Alden shoved to his feet, and would have stalked out of the pub, but Percy caught his hand.

"Where are you going?"

"I don't know. I just know we have to help Jackie. He helped us, even though he had to know it might not end well for him." Alden turned to Xava. "Do you know where he might be?"

"Rumour has it he was brought to Beasor." Xava held up her hand to stop Alden from asking. "I don't know where he is, except he's in the capital somewhere."

"Fuck," Chal cursed. "That's a rather large area to start searching."

"I have to get back to the hospital. It was nice seeing you again, Steril. Maybe we can meet for coffee while I'm here."

"Certainly, Xava." Steril stood and escorted the Gypsy out of the pub.

"The only people who should be upset with Jackie were Karl and Roscoe. As far as I know, there weren't any other people involved in my kidnapping." Percy tapped his fingers against his lips.

"Maybe there was someone getting a cut from those assholes' winnings. Someone who knew they were using Percy, and what Percy could do, but didn't care about it. If Jackie really is in Catalai, then it was obviously a Beasor who did it." Chal looked like he wanted to punch something.

"It sounds like something a Thief would be involved in," Steril spoke up, looking sick to his stomach. "Again, we're taught not to care about who we hurt as long as we get what we want. God, I hate being a Thief."

Percy reached out and took Steril's hand in his. Alden dropped his hand on Steril's shoulder.

"We trust you, Steril. To change up what Xava said a little, not all Thieves are bad. Admittedly, most of them have no morals, or care about taking from people, but there are a few who do care." Percy grimaced. "Not all magical Beasors are selfish and uncaring, but each of our kind has some. It's a fact of life."

"Right." Chal stood. "I'm going to see if I can get a hold of Digs and Visi. I want to know exactly how hard they looked, and what, if anything, they found while looking for Jackie."

Steril stood as well. "I'll walk out with you. I'm going back to the facility to see what I can find there. If that doesn't work, I'll send out messages on my network to see if anything pops up on that."

"Thanks, guys. We'll meet at the coffee shop Steril likes in the morning to see what everyone has."

"I might not be able to make it. I only get so much leave, and I'm reaching my limit soon." Steril frowned.

"Then send the information with someone you trust that can meet us there," Alden told him. "We don't know for sure how long Jackie's been here, and, from all the stuff I've ever heard, humans don't do well on Beasor. Their lungs aren't meant to breathe our air."

"Probably too clean for them," Percy quipped.

Alden rolled his eyes, and shook hands with the Tramp and Thief. He grabbed Percy's hand, and dragged him upstairs, trusting that Greta was all right running the bar on her own.

They got into the apartment, and Alden dropped to the couch, bracing his elbows on his knees and burying his face in his hands. Percy sat next to him, rubbing his back.

"Hey, it's not our fault Jackie got taken," Percy said.

"Yes, it is. Vis and Digs should have helped him while the other Tramps took Roscoe and Karl to the Sublant universe. Jackie should never have been left alone."

"How were they to know that someone would kidnap Jackie? As far as any of us knew, they were working alone. Beasors rarely interact with humans. I mean, even Thieves think humans are beneath them." Percy ran his hand down Alden's back.

Alden took a deep breath, and exhaled. "I know, but I can't help think of how scared Jackie is right now."

"Probably as scared as I was when I was on Earth," Percy admitted.

"Right, even more so because he won't understand anything about our world, Percy. He might have known who or what you were, but he doesn't know what our world is, or what our people can do."

Percy leant back against the cushions, and Alden turned to see him staring across the room. The thoughtful expression on Percy's face told Alden his lover was rummaging through old thoughts and memories. At times, Alden thought Percy had a photographic memory, because the Gypsy never forgot anything.

Alden got up and started making dinner. Percy would speak up when he'd sorted things out in his brain. He'd just got the food on the table when Percy joined him in the kitchen.

"I think he knew me, Alden." Sitting at the table, Percy frowned at his plate.

"Who knew you? Jackie?"

Percy nodded. "Yes. When he snuck in to talk to me, he asked me who I was. I told him, and he swore. It was then he told me he'd get me out of there."

Alden took a bite of food while he thought about Percy's revelation. He set his fork down. "How would a human know who you were? You've never really interacted with them before, have you?"

"I know. It doesn't make any sense." A sudden thought must have hit Percy because he stopped and his face went white. "What if Jackie wasn't human? What if he was a Thief? What if some Thief had stolen his soul and identity to play among the humans for a while? He could have done that, and egged Karl and Roscoe on."

"But why have them kidnap a Gypsy? Why would he do that? He had to have known the humans would use you until you died." Alden shook his head. "It doesn't make sense."

"I know that, but it's possible. He might not have thought it through, then he saw me, and he started to freak out slightly. After I told him my name, he really freaked out because he recognised it."

Alden thought about Percy's theory as they ate. He wasn't sure Percy was right, but it made as much sense as anything else did. They rinsed the dishes, and filled the dishwasher. After starting it, they went back into the living room, Percy with some wine, and Alden a beer.

They settled back on the couch, with Percy curled into Alden's side. He rested his chin on Percy's head, and sighed.

"If you're right, we need to find out who did it, Percy. They need to be punished by the High Council. You could have gotten killed, and no non-Beasor can ever know what Gypsies, Tramps, or Thieves can do." Alden hugged Percy close. "You might have died, and he needs to pay for that."

Percy nodded, his soft hair rubbing against Alden's chin. "Yes, I realise that. What if he's young, though, and doesn't really know any better? Hell, you know what they teach Thieves at the facility."

"Thieves have never been known for their ability to know right from wrong," Alden mentioned, eyes closed as he savoured Percy's warmth.

"Neither are any of the magical Beasors. Most have used their power for less than good reasons." Percy snuggled closer.

"Hmm..." Alden had lost track of the conversation. All he wanted to think about was Percy in his arms, under him, or over him. Alden wasn't picky.

He eased Percy back and lifted his chin, placing a kiss on Percy's plump lips. Percy wound his arms around Alden's shoulders, and wiggled until he straddled Alden's lap. They kissed for several minutes, simply revelling in the fact that they were together. Alden cupped Percy's butt in his hands, squeezing hard enough to bruise Percy's flesh.

Percy began rocking their groins together, and Alden pulled his mouth away from Percy's lips to trail biting kisses along his jaw to his neck. Alden smiled against Percy's skin as his lover tipped his head to give Alden more access to his throat.

He gasped when Percy pushed down the waistbands of their pants, and their erections met skin to skin. Percy wrapped his hand around both of their dicks, and they began moving, fucking Percy's hand. Alden ran his fingers down from the dimple at the top of Percy's ass to his puckered ring. He caressed his finger over Percy's hole once, and Percy jerked.

Alden brought his finger up to press it against Percy's lips, and his lover sucked it in, coating it with spit while they continued to drive each other higher and higher. When Alden thought it was wet enough, he removed his finger from Percy's mouth and returned it to Percy's hole, pressing in an inch at a time until it was buried to the knuckle.

Percy arched, pushing back onto Alden's finger and thrusting forward into his hand, bringing more friction to their lovemaking. Alden encouraged Percy to angle his hips some more, so he could nail Percy's gland with every push in.

"Oh, God, Alden!" Percy cried out as Alden hit the right spot.

"Come on, honey. You can let go. I'll catch you when you fall. I'll always be here," Alden whispered against Percy's ear as he played with Percy's ass.

Percy's grip tightened on their cocks to an almost painful pressure, but it was more than enough to push Alden over the edge. He made sure to take Percy with him. Their cum splashed over Percy's hand, and their groins. They shuddered and trembled in each other's arms while their climaxes slowly faded away. Percy tugged their pants back into place.

Alden encircled Percy's waist, and stood. Percy squeaked and wrapped his legs around Alden before Alden carried him down the hallway to the shower.

"We'll clean up, and head to bed. Nothing can be fixed tonight," Alden suggested as he set Percy on the counter in the bathroom, and turned to start the water running.

Percy leaned against the mirror, watching Alden move about the room. He didn't say anything, and Alden wasn't sure if it was because Percy was tired or if Percy was thinking about things. Either way, Alden wasn't interested in talking about Jackie, or anything else, at the moment. He wanted to clean up, and go to bed.

"You're right, but I need to meditate before I go to bed." Percy jumped off the sink and stripped.

Alden appreciated the lean lines of his lover's body, and, even though he'd just come, his cock took a small interest in Percy's nakedness. He quickly took off his pants, and joined Percy in the shower. He moaned as the hot water cascaded over his body, easing muscles and rinsing off the sweat from the day.

Percy took pity on him and soaped Alden up, letting the water wash the suds away. Alden reciprocated, and they showered quickly, which didn't always happen when the two of them took a shower together. Usually, they'd play around until the water ran cold.

They finished up getting ready for bed, and Percy padded down the hallway to his old room. He'd turned it into his meditation room, and Alden didn't have a problem with that. As long as Percy kept sharing his bed, Alden didn't care how many rooms Percy claimed as his own.

Alden climbed into bed, and punched his pillow into the correct shape before closing his eyes. He must have drifted off to sleep, because he never felt Percy come to bed. Percy hitting him in the side woke him up.

Sitting up, he glanced over at his lover, and noticed Percy's eyes were closed. *Must be dreaming*, Alden thought, but he ducked as Percy swung out to hit him again. Alden caught Percy's fist, and leaned over him.

"Hey, Percy, wake up. You're having a nightmare." He rested his hand on Percy's shoulder and shook him.

"Get away from me, you bastard." Percy struck out with his other hand, but Alden dodged it.

"Come on, honey. Wake up, because I don't want you to give me a black eye."

After a couple more shakes, Percy opened his eyes and blinked as he stared up at Alden. After making sure Percy wasn't going to attack him, Alden reached out to turn the lamp beside the bed on. Once the soft light eased the darkness away from the bed, Percy went white and sat up. He took Alden's face in his hands, and studied him.

"I didn't hit you or anything, did I?"

"Well, once, but it didn't hurt, so we're good." Alden brushed a lock of hair off Percy's forehead. "What were you dreaming about?"

Percy shrugged and scrubbed his hands over his face. "I don't know. I guess I was back in that room with those bastards raping me."

Alden frowned. "Why won't you go talk to someone about your experiences, Percy? I mean, I'm sure you think you've dealt with it all, but something tells me you need to work it out by telling someone who doesn't have anything invested in you except as a patient."

"What do you mean by that?" Percy stared at Alden.

"You won't talk to me about it in any great detail, because you don't want to appear weak in front of me. While you seem to have dealt with the whole sex issue, there are other problems you need to think about and acknowledge." Alden leant forward and kissed Percy. "I'm not a professional, and I want you to not be afraid anymore."

Percy took a deep breath, and nodded. "You're right. I'll call someone tomorrow and set up an appointment."

"Thank you."

Alden pulled Percy into his arms, and they lay together. He left the light on. It didn't bother him, and he knew it helped Percy feel safer. Soon, Percy relaxed in his arms, falling asleep, and Alden wasn't far behind him.

Chapter Eleven

Percy took a bite of his muffin, enjoying the way the flavour burst in his mouth. Both Chal and Alden chuckled, and he rolled his eyes at them. He didn't care if he sounded like he was having the best sex of his life, because the muffin was damn good.

The other two sipped their coffee, not inclined to talk so early in the morning. Percy shook his head. It really wasn't that early, but for Alden, who worked in the bar most nights, eight in the morning was a time he rarely saw. Yet Steril told them he could get away from the facility for an hour around then, so there they were at the coffee shop.

"When's the Thief getting here?" Chal asked, shoving his cup around the table.

"He said he'd be here as close to eight as he could get. It's hard for Thieves to get out of the facility, and his teachers will want to know who he's talking to and what he's doing." Alden frowned. "Thieves are the most secretive of you magical Beasors."

"I know, and it's annoying at times," Chal commented.

Percy wiped all the crumbs from his face, and dropped his napkin on his used plate. "Just give him a few minutes. No one really knows where the facility is, so we have no idea how long it takes to get from there to here."

"Did you guys think about the situation? Do you have an idea where Jackie might be on Beasor?" Chal glanced at them.

Percy and Alden looked at each other, and Alden grimaced.

"We talked about it. We'd rather wait until Steril gets here, so we don't have to repeat it."

Alden reached over and took Percy's hand in his. Percy smiled at how comforting and familiar Alden's touch had become. It was something Percy never wanted to be without again.

"Is your magic coming back?" Chal signalled for another cup of coffee.

Percy shrugged. "Not completely yet. There are sparks, but it's not all there. I just keep doing what I need to do to get it back. I'm sure it'll appear soon."

Alden snorted, and Percy chuckled. Oh, hell yeah, they would continue doing what was needed to get his magic back. It wasn't like they were going to stop having sex any time soon. It was the reason why Percy hadn't panicked when his magic hadn't come back as quickly as he'd have liked.

Chal studied them for a moment, but, when they didn't say anything else, he let it go. "Good to hear. I'm sure you'll be back to normal soon enough."

What was normal? Percy doubted he'd ever go back to the way he was before he was captured. Yet, if he could get the nightmares under control, he'd be good. Most of them woke him up, but he would manage to get out of bed without bothering Alden. Last night's was the first to be bad enough for him to strike out.

He thought about the promise he'd made Alden about finding someone to talk to about his experiences. He'd keep it, even if it was difficult to tell anyone what had happened to him. Percy hated anyone knowing he was stupid enough to get caught by two humans whose IQs matched Percy's shoe size.

"Sorry to make you wait, everyone." Steril dropped into the empty chair at the table and exhaled sharply. "I ran from the sled stop, and, boy, I'm out of shape. Going to have to start exercising."

The barista brought over a steaming mug of coffee and a plate with two muffins on it. Steril smiled his thanks, and slid one of the muffins onto Percy's plate. Percy didn't even think about protesting. Those muffins were like the best drugs in all the universes. Steril took a drink of his coffee before looking at his watch.

"I have an hour and a half before I have to leave. It was really hard to get permission from my teachers to come into the city today. They have been acting strange for the past two days."

Alden and Percy exchanged another glance, and Alden gestured for Percy to tell them the theory he'd come up with. He took a breath, and nodded.

"What if Jackie was actually a Thief?"

Chal and Steril looked surprised, but Percy stayed silent, letting them work through it in their minds.

Finally, Chal spoke. "I guess it could be possible."

Steril looked confused. "I'm not sure what a Thief would have gotten out of the whole thing."

"My thought is that the Thief took Jackie's personality, or whatever. I'm not entirely sure how it works. Anyway, he goes to Earth to play around, mess with the stupid humans. He gets involved with Roscoe and Karl. Has them convinced he's harmless, but somehow he's pulling the strings behind the scenes." Percy paused to take a sip of his coffee. "He could have been the one who told them about what Gypsies can do."

"But he seemed scared of those two. Also, he said he had to help you because of what Roscoe and Karl did to a female Gypsy," Chal pointed out.

Alden leant forward. "Right, but that could have been a lie. Percy said Jackie seemed to recognise him, once he found out what Percy's name was. I think he didn't care what the humans did with Percy, until he realised who Percy was."

Steril still didn't look convinced. "If he did know who Percy was, why didn't he just come back here on his own and tell us where Percy was?"

"Because the High Council would have arrested him for what he'd done. While Thieves are given leniency for a lot of what they do, stealing a human's identity and causing the capture of another Beasor, especially one of the magical ones, is punishable by death." Alden gestured wildly.

"It's why Jackie has disappeared. The Thief comes back to Beasor, returns to his normal life, and none the wiser." Percy pushed his plate away from him. "It's the perfect crime, in many ways."

"I still don't understand why any Beasor would be willing to allow humans to torture one of his fellow magic users." Steril shook his head.

Chal reached over, and patted Steril's hand. "It's because you're a nice guy, Steril. You wouldn't dream of doing something like that to someone, but there are people out there who don't have a problem using people, if it furthers their agenda."

"True." Steril played with his cup while he thought. "If what you think is true, that could explain why the teachers at the facility are acting weird. Maybe they discovered what the Thief was doing, and they're trying to figure out what to do with him or her."

Percy and Alden agreed. Chal grimaced as he stood.

"I have to go, but I'll put out some feelers. I know a few people who are around the High Council. They might have heard something. I'll let you know if I discover anything."

Chal nodded to all of them before he left. Percy, Alden and Steril sat, staring at each other.

"What do we do if we discover Percy's theory is true? Do we go to the Council and tell them?" Steril didn't seem eager to do that.

"We'd have to know who exactly the perpetrator was before we did anything."

"Then we approach someone close to the Council that we trust." Alden scrubbed his hand over his face. "I've only met the Chairman of the High Council once, and he was trying to blend in with the crowd here. Being a pub owner doesn't get me into the top levels of Catalai society."

"Actually, you'd be surprised, Alden. Several High Council members come to your pub to drink. Also, several top level officials come as well," Percy spoke up. "Your pub is a popular hang-out for magical Beasors, and the Council likes to take advantage of that."

Alden's eyes widened in shock at Percy's revelation. "Really? I had no idea anyone important in the government came to my place on a regular basis."

"Most of them are repeat customers," Percy commented.

"You're going to have to point them out to me,"
Alden ordered. "I won't make a big deal about them,
but I want to make sure Reagan and his bouncers
know when Council members are at the pub. To keep
an extra eye on them."

"I will." Percy turned to look at Steril. "Does it
bother you, knowing one of your fellow Thieves might
be responsible for something like this?"

Steril didn't lift his gaze from the table. "Well, it
bothers me, but I can't say I'll be surprised if it turns
out you're right. I told you, the teachers at the facility
don't teach ethics or morals to Thieves. Most of us will
get jobs stealing things for people, so why would you
make sure your Thief had a conscience before you
hired him?"

"True. People who have morals usually don't make
good Thieves," Alden admitted.

"I'm still not sure if I believe you or not," Steril
confessed as he looked up to meet Percy's gaze.

"I know, and that's fine, Steril. You don't have to
believe me just because we're friends. It was the only
theory that made sense to me, especially with the
rumour that Jackie was on Beasor. Humans don't
come here unless a Beasor brings them here. I can't
think of anyone who would go to find Jackie. None of
my family would, and Chal's friends would have
helped him out, but kept him on Earth." Percy
stretched. "I think we need to take a walk. You still
have time before you head back, right?"

Steril nodded.

"Good. We'll make our way back to the sled stop
you need to take back to the facility."

"This really isn't the best part of town to wander
around in," Alden spoke up, but he stood, offering
Percy his hand.

"True, but if I stay here, I'm going to have another muffin, and, while I might need to gain more weight, I don't need to eat three muffins in one sitting."

They laughed as they paid and wandered out of the coffee shop. Steril gestured in the direction of his sled stop.

"If you don't like being a Thief, why are you at the facility?" Alden asked as they walked.

"All Thieves must be trained in how to control their magic. The majority of us have the minor powers, where we take objects. Some of us can take on personalities or looks, and become a copy of the person we've stolen them from. The most powerful Thieves can steal souls."

Percy shuddered at the thought of someone stealing his soul. "Then whoever's soul was stolen would cease to exist, and the Thief would retain all the traits or powers of the person. Right?"

Steril nodded. "It's not a very nice power to have. Of course, all the stealing comes at a high price. If a Thief uses his or her powers, they're debilitated for days, sucked dry of power and strength. That's what makes me question why the Thief would do something like that. If he did, there has to be another reason why he did it, as the cost is too high to do it on a whim."

Percy hadn't known about how much strength it took to steal something. He wanted to slap his forehead. It made sense because he couldn't use his powers without becoming tired for a day or two, and stealing was far more work than what he did.

Alden slid his arm around Percy's waist, drawing him closer to Alden as they walked. Steril looked unhappy, and Percy couldn't resist asking him.

"So, do you have a boyfriend, Steril?"

Steril blushed, like Percy had figured he would, and shook his head. "No. Most people stay away from me. I'm not really boyfriend material."

"Not boyfriend material?" Alden grunted. "Are you kidding me? If I hadn't already fallen in love with Percy, I'd be chasing after you like Percy after those muffins."

Percy elbowed Alden and glared at him when his lover shot a smile in his direction.

"What? I'm telling the truth. I thought you were going to make love to the first muffin you had this morning." Alden laughed as Percy punched him in the arm.

Percy slipped away from Alden's embrace, and went to join arms with Steril. "Ignore the whole muffin thing, but Alden is right. You're really cute. Why wouldn't a guy want to latch on to you?"

"Probably because my father is a complete ass, and no one wants to deal with him." Steril gazed at Percy. "And I'm not very good-looking or anything. Rather ordinary for a Thief."

"And Percy is ordinary for a Gypsy, and I'm rather plain for a regular Beasor. Yet we all have something that makes us special." Alden hesitated as he thought. "Okay, maybe I don't have anything making me special, but both you and Percy do."

"Who's your father?" Percy wanted to know who Steril's father was, and why he'd scare off potential boyfriends. It didn't make sense. Hell, Percy's father was a complete asshole, but it hadn't scared Alden away.

"I don't want to talk about him." Steril shut the door on that line of questioning. "It doesn't matter anyway. I'd rather be alone than having to worry about making someone else happy. I'm good at disappointing people."

"Something tells me that's your father talking," Alden guessed.

"He's said it a few times," Steril confessed.

"Fathers can be the bane of our existence. Trust me, I know." Percy sympathised with Steril's unhappiness with his father.

"I wouldn't know. I never met my father. All I know is I must have had one, right? Since I couldn't have been hatched, or anything like that."

Alden's outburst brought Percy and Steril to a halt. Both of them stared at Alden for a moment, and Percy felt ashamed. He knew Alden hadn't known who his parents were, yet he'd gone on about how much he didn't like his family. Just because Alden accepted that not every family was perfect, he probably would still like to know who his parents were.

"Sorry, love." He leant forward to brush a kiss over Alden's lips.

"No, I'm sorry. I didn't mean to burst out like that." Alden dropped his gaze to the sidewalk under their feet.

"Come on." Steril grabbed Percy's hand and tugged. "There's a candy store I want to stop at before I have to go back to the facility."

"Great. More ways to make me fat," Percy groused, but didn't try to stop Steril.

Alden laughed. "Just gives me more of you to love."

Percy glared over his shoulder at Alden, and his lover winked back at him. He finally smiled, because he couldn't stay mad at Alden for long. He never could be upset for more than a day with anyone. It wasn't in his nature to brood or sulk. Percy might throw a tantrum or pout, but he rarely stayed mad.

They spent the next half hour in a small candy store, buying candy for Alden's employees, and Percy ordered a dozen chocolate-covered strawberries to be delivered to Kiki. It was a thank-you for letting him stay with her while he got his head out of his ass. Also, strawberries were a rare delicacy from the human universe, and Kiki would love the fact that he had spent so much money on her.

Percy hugged Steril when they got to the sled stop. "We'll keep you in the loop as we work on trying to figure all this out. Also, let us know if you find anything else."

"I will, and thank you for hanging out with me. I think this is the first time I've spent time with anyone who wasn't a classmate." Steril grinned as he hugged Alden as well.

"Any time, Steril. You know you're welcome at the pub whenever you want to come by. Also, we're more than willing to meet you for dinner or breakfast," Alden said when they stepped away from each other.

The sled pulled up to the stop, and Steril waved as he climbed in. They waited until the sled was out of sight before flagging down their own sled to take them back to their apartment.

They settled into the back seat, and Percy rested his head on Alden's shoulder.

"Who do you think Steril's father is?"

"Doesn't matter to me. All that matters is it sounds like the guy is an asshole like your dad." Alden rubbed his cheek against Percy's hair.

"Certainly does. Must be something about fathers who are magical."

"Maybe."

"Have you ever tried to find out who your parents were?" Percy wasn't sure how Alden would react to his asking, but Percy had to try.

Alden stiffened slightly, but didn't pull away. "I tried when I turned eighteen, but there weren't any records of a birth on the day I was born, or on the day the nurses guessed I was probably born."

Percy thought about it for a second. "Oh my God, that's right. You wouldn't know your true birthday, because no one knew who your parents were."

"Right, so the nurses made a guess and wrote it down on the forms. It's the day I celebrate every year anyway." Alden's shrug lifted Percy's head a little. "I've gotten over it, for the most part. It only really bothers me on the holidays, because everyone else is celebrating them with their families, and I don't have anyone to spend the day with."

Percy sat up straight and poked Alden in the chest. "You do now. There won't be a holiday or special day from now on that you'll be alone on. In addition to me, you have Chal, Steril, and all your employees. I'm pretty sure they consider themselves part of your family."

Alden rubbed the spot Percy had nailed with his finger. "Ow! Okay, don't do that again. You're right. I do have you and friends to be my family. That's why I tend not to worry about it anymore."

Percy returned to his favourite spot, which being wrapped in Alden's arms. He laid his hand on Alden's chest, pressing his palm flat to feel Alden's heartbeat.

"Where did you grow up, if you didn't have a family?"

Beasor didn't have orphanages. They had workhouses for the non-magical Beasors, and for the magical ones there were schools or foster families willing to take them in. It seemed like a harsh life for those ordinary Beasors.

"When I was old enough, I was sent to a workhouse. They found a job for me right away as a bar sweep. I'd go to work at eight in the morning, and sweep out the bars along Granted Avenue until they opened at nine in the evening. They were long days, but I really didn't mind. At least I wasn't on the streets, begging for a living."

Percy wanted to agree with Alden, but he really didn't think working for such long hours as a child was a good thing. It would explain Alden's work ethic, though. Alden spent a lot of time every day doing work for the pub. Percy couldn't complain, though, since Alden never ignored or forgot about him. Also, if Percy asked, Alden would drop everything to help him.

The sled slowed to a stop in front of Alden's pub, and they climbed out after Alden had slid his card to pay for the ride. They went upstairs, and Percy dropped on their couch, his mind whirling with everything they'd discussed already that morning.

Alden kissed his cheek. "I have to go down and place some orders. Why don't you meditate for a little while before looking up a therapist to talk to about what happened?"

Percy sighed. "Sounds good, love. I'll talk to you at lunch?"

"Of course. You can come down and we'll go out, or we can make something here. I'm easy either way."

Percy leered at his lover. "Yes, you are."

Laughing, Alden shook his head. "I'm out of here. Try not to make yourself crazy over-thinking things, Percy. It'll work out eventually."

Percy waved Alden out of the room, and stood. He wandered down the hall, leaving a trail of clothes behind him. He entered his old bedroom and sat on the floor, crossing his legs and resting his hands, palms up, on his thighs.

Taking deep breaths, Percy slowly began to clear his mind of any questions, thoughts or worries he might have had. The best way to meditate was to empty his mind, and breathe. He closed his eyes, rocking ever so slightly to establish a rhythm to let his heart beat to.

Soon he'd sunk into a deep trance, where he gathered his power threads carefully. Too hard a tug could damage one irrevocably. He smiled when he held several in his hands. It was a good sign to see so many.

Percy still didn't have enough to perform any big magic, but he had enough, and he wasn't worried he'd lose all of his power. Percy wove the threads into a basket of magic, which would hold the rest of his power as it grew and pooled in his soul. He hoped he'd never get so close to losing it again.

Once he'd finished with that, he cautiously exited his meditation. Percy had to do it with a great deal of care. There were stories of Gypsies being caught in their meditations and never coming back to themselves. No one understood how that happened, either.

Percy frowned. Now that he'd thought of it, there was a lot about Beasor magic people didn't know. Even those who used it the most were horribly uninformed about their powers. No wonder so many dangerous things happened, and people only had rumours to help them fix what was wrong.

He stretched as he returned to the present world. Percy waited a few minutes for the fog to leave his

mind entirely before he stood. After grabbing a
change of clothes, he headed into the bathroom to take
a very hot shower. It eased whichever muscles were
sore from sitting for so long.

After drying and dressing, he grabbed some juice
from the refrigerator and went to the living room,
snatching up the phone as he went by. When he had
everything arranged just as he liked it, he flipped open
the screen on the phone, and typed in therapists. It
searched through the listings to find numbers for him.

Each one he brought up had a small video
commercial attached to it. Percy watched every one
until he found one that sounded like she would fit
what he needed. He'd figured out that he wasn't
interested in going to a male therapist. Again, it
probably had to do with not appearing weak in front
of them, as Alden had mentioned the night before.

He hit the dial button, and waited.

"Hello, this is Dr Mulles' office. How may I help
you?"

The doctor's receptionist looked competent and
attractive. Percy smiled.

"Is the doctor accepting new patients?"

"Yes. Would you like to make an appointment?"

Percy did, and set one up for the next day. After
giving the receptionist all his information, he hung up,
and set the phone aside. He wasn't sure how he felt
about going to tell some stranger about his problems,
but it had to be done. Mostly because he didn't want
to beat Alden up every night while he slept.

He curled up on the couch, and let his mind drift.
Working with his magic, even while meditating, tired
him out still, so he always ended up taking a nap
afterwards. It was the main reason why he usually

meditated at night, and could head right to bed with Alden.

Percy's eyes closed, and he fell asleep, his mind clear of nightmares for the moment.

Chapter Twelve

Alden looked up as Percy walked into the apartment. He wanted to ask right away how the therapy session had gone, but, when Percy passed him and headed to his meditation room, Alden decided to let Percy tell him in his own time.

He bet it was probably really hard for Percy to open up and tell anyone what had happened. It wasn't that Alden didn't want to hear what Percy had gone through, but he really did think Percy wouldn't want to appear weak or less than a man in front of him. It would never happen. Alden didn't think less of Percy for his capture.

Alden went back to cooking dinner. He'd dish up a plate for Percy, and put it in the oven to keep warm. He wasn't going to interrupt his lover's trance, if that was what Percy needed to feel better.

Percy had seemed happy yesterday as they went to bed. He'd talked about his magic coming back and that soon it would be at full power again. Alden was happy for his lover, knowing Percy wouldn't have been the same bright, happy person he used to be without it.

Of course, Percy had changed. He wasn't as flighty as he had been. Percy had his serious moments, which again Alden understood. Alden really did hope that the therapist would help Percy.

He got his plate ready, and put Percy's in the stove. After sitting at the table, he started eating. Alden had two hours before he needed to get downstairs to help Greta with the customers. It was a Friday night, and the pub would be packed, plus he liked being down there on busy nights. Chatting with regulars and meeting new customers were things Alden liked.

The phone rang as Alden was rinsing his plate. He grabbed it off the counter, headed into the living room, and flipped it open as he flopped onto the couch.

"Hey there, Steril. What's up?"

Steril didn't look well.

"Are you okay?"

"I'm fine," Steril said, his eyes red and swollen like he'd been crying.

"You don't look fine, but you probably can't tell me if something's wrong." Alden frowned.

"I'm fine. I wanted to let you know I'll be coming to see you tonight. Can you make sure Percy and Chal are there?"

"Sure. When do you plan on being here?" Alden would leave a note for Percy if his lover wasn't done meditating by the time he left.

"I should be there about eleven." Steril glanced up at something out of sight of Alden. "I have to go now. I'll see you later."

The screen went black, and Alden shut the phone. He set it on the end table before stretching out on the couch. He folded his arms behind his head, and stared up at the ceiling for a moment.

Something was bothering Steril, and Alden had a feeling it had to do with Percy's hostage situation. He hoped Steril wasn't getting in trouble for looking into things for them. He remembered he needed to let Chal know to show up at the pub.

Alden picked the phone up and sent Chal a quick text. He returned it to the table, and settled in for a short nap. He'd got up early to see Percy off to his appointment, and he'd need to rest a little bit before he stayed up until four in the morning when the pub closed.

"Honey, you need to wake up."

Grunting, Alden wrinkled his nose as he tried to remember where the hell he was. He hated waking up someplace other than his bed.

"Come on. It's almost time for you to open the pub. I'm sure Greta and the others are going to start showing up soon."

Alden frowned, but opened his eyes to find Percy crouched by the couch. Percy smiled at him, and brushed his hair off his forehead.

"Hey, there. You need to change and head downstairs." Percy gave him a kiss on the cheek.

"I will."

Alden sat up, and swung his legs over the side of the couch. Percy moved to sit next to him.

"Chal sent a text saying he'd be here at eleven. Why did he want us to know?" Percy rubbed Alden's shoulders.

"Oh, Steril called while you were meditating. He wants to meet all of us at eleven at the pub. He didn't look good—I think he's found out something about Jackie."

Percy nodded. "I thought that might be why Chal was telling us when he was going to be here. The Tramp usually just shows up, not warning us beforehand."

Alden stood and stretched, wincing as his back cracked and creaked. "How long was I asleep?"

"Only about thirty minutes, I think." Percy stood next to him.

He encircled Percy's waist, pulling his lover close for a deep kiss. He stroked his tongue along Percy's, eliciting a groan. Alden sighed, and eased a few inches away.

"Sorry. Didn't mean to start anything I can't finish right now. Greta called me earlier, and she's going to be late tonight." Alden nuzzled Percy's jaw quickly before dashing down the hallway. "How'd did your therapy session go?"

He yelled the last question as he stripped out of his lounging pants and loose shirt. He tossed them towards the laundry basket before grabbing a pair of tight pants out of the closet. Alden was buttoning them when Percy strolled into the room.

"It went well for being the first one, I guess." Percy shrugged as he propped his back against one of their dressers. "I'm going back again next week. You were right, though."

"What do you mean?" He tugged a form-fitting black short-sleeved shirt on, smoothing it down over his stomach.

"You were right about me talking to someone about my emotions from being held captive. I can tell it's already helped a little. After I meditated, I could tell my magic is getting stronger. I might be able to let the Gypsy Councilman know I can take jobs again soon."

Alden cradled Percy's face, and kissed him. "I'm so happy for you, Percy. I know you didn't like not being able to pull your weight around here, but I don't care. You're healing still, and I'll support you as long as need be, for you to get well."

Percy kissed him back before pinching him on the ass. "Thanks. Now get out of here. I'm going to eat the food you left in the oven for me, and take a shower. I'll be down at eleven to see what Steril has to say."

"See you then."

Alden went to the front door, and stomped into his boots before heading downstairs. He got the door unlocked before the rest of his employees arrived. They got the chairs and tables set, and the glasses cleaned and lined up. Everything was in place when the first customers showed up, and the race was on.

It was a good thing breathing was a natural reflex, or Alden wouldn't have had time to even do that. Around eleven that night, he saw Steril wind his way through the crowd to the table Chal sat at. Greta had come in a few minutes earlier, so she was able to take over for him behind the bar.

"Greta, I'm taking a break," he called out as Percy appeared at the end of the counter.

She waved at him, and he slipped out to join Percy in the crowd. They made their way through all the customers, stopping every so often to talk to people who wanted to tell Alden how much they enjoyed the pub. He was polite, but he wanted to get to the table as soon as possible.

"Have you guys ordered?" he asked as they arrived at the table, and sat.

"Yeah. Your staff's good, Alden. In fact, she's already on her way back." Chal nodded towards the waitress making her way to them.

Alden waited until their drinks were delivered and the waitress had left before he braced his elbows on the table and looked at Steril.

"What have you found out?"

Steril's gaze dropped to the table, but only for a second before he looked back up. He met each of their gazes, and he nodded.

"From everything I've discovered, Percy's theory is right. Jackie was a Thief. The only good thing is he didn't steal anyone's soul to become Jackie, but he did take Jackie's personality and his life."

Percy snorted, and Steril shrugged.

"I know. There doesn't seem to be much difference between the two, but there is. If he'd stolen Jackie's soul, Jackie would have ceased to be. By stealing his personality, he was able to take over Jackie's life long enough to do all the damage he did."

Alden thought about it. "I guess I can see what you're saying. Doesn't mean I agree with you, but I see how you can think that."

"I don't think that," Steril protested. "All the teachers at the facility think it, and so, once they find the Thief who did this, his punishment will be less than death."

Alden almost shot to his feet, but Percy grabbed his arm to keep him seated. "Less than death? After what his meddling did to Percy? How can that be?"

"Again, it's what I've discovered, and don't ask who told me because I can't say." Steril's jaw set in a stubborn line.

"Okay. We won't ask you, though I'll do my damnedest to find out the truth," Chal warned him.

Steril nodded. "I wouldn't expect anything else."

Alden tapped Steril on the hand and brought the Thief's attention back to him. "What else have you discovered?"

"He's young, and, actually, he was trying to exact revenge." Steril took a sip of his juice.

Alden narrowed his eyes. "Revenge? Do you mean the story about the female Gypsy being used, killed, and discarded was true?"

"I believe so," Steril agreed. "From everything I've heard, it was someone he loved, and she disappeared one day when she'd flashed to Earth. He searched for her all over the planet, but he couldn't find her. Unfortunately, when he did find her, she was dead. It took him years until he learnt Roscoe and Karl were the ones responsible for her death."

"I'd want to kill them," Charl muttered.

"So would I," Alden agreed, putting his arm around Percy's shoulders and holding his lover close.

"Maybe, but I think he was setting them up for being punished. What I don't think was that he planned on them actually finding another Gypsy, and said Gypsy being Percy Harlow. You might not like your father, but he is a very important person in Beasor politics. People know who he is."

"So when Percy told him his name, the guy panicked and did everything he could to let someone know Percy was being held," Alden muttered.

"Right. Again, from what I heard, he told Xava because he knew she'd be able to get the word to someone who would be able to help. Maybe he knew she was a Gypsy herself. Maybe he didn't. He told her, and hung around until Percy was rescued. He also stayed around until Roscoe and Karl got their punishment."

"Then he disappeared back to Beasor, planning on never saying a word about what he did, and the damage he caused Percy." Alden curled his lip in disgust.

Steril nodded. "But someone figured it out, and told the teachers. They confronted him, and he confessed."

"Yet no one is going to come and tell Percy anything? They were just going to let him continue to suffer because this kid decided to extract his own revenge on some stupid humans. Why didn't he just steal their souls? Wouldn't that have been a more fitting revenge than to allow them to have the opportunity to do it to someone else?"

Steril looked like he was going to be sick. Alden didn't want to make the Thief feel bad, because it was like killing the messenger, and he understood he shouldn't be upset with Steril. His friend was just doing what he could, to make sure to keep them in the loop without giving away his source of information.

"I'm sorry, Steril. Thank you for letting us know. I might not like what you told us, but that's my problem, not yours."

Percy stood, and went over to Steril. He embraced the younger man, hugging him tight.

"Believe me. As much as I hate what happened to me and want the person who allowed it to happen punished, I know it wasn't your fault. You're only telling us what you know."

Steril pushed his face into Percy's shirt and shuddered for a moment. Was knowing what this other Thief had done that upsetting to Steril? Alden had never seen one of the magical Beasors act like Steril when one of their fellows chose to break the rules.

"I have to go," Steril said as he stepped away from Percy. He wiped his eyes, and nodded to Chal and Alden before he left.

Percy dropped back into his chair, and folded his arms. "Shit. He's taking it harder than I am, and I'm the person all the crap happened to."

"I know. Maybe it's someone he knows and trusted," Alden suggested.

"I'm going to find out who it was. I warned Steril I would, and, when I do, I'm going to keep an eye on the Thief to make sure he doesn't do it again." Chal finished his ale in one large gulp. He slammed his mug onto the table and stood. "I have to go. Got a job, so I'll be seeing you sometime next week."

"Take care and be safe, Chal." Alden shook the Tramp's hand, and watched Chal make his way out of the pub. "I guess that went well, all things considered."

Percy snorted. "It could have been worse, I guess. Chal could've decided Steril was the one who did it, and beat him up."

Alden shot a glance at Percy. "Did the thought cross your mind?"

"Of course it did, and don't try to tell me you didn't think the exact same thing." Percy poked Alden in the side. "It would be the perfect explanation, but…"

"Yeah, but Steril doesn't strike me as the type of guy who would do something like that. He would try to bring Roscoe and Karl to justice in their own world, instead of letting the Tramps deal out their own form of twisted justice." Alden shoved to his feet. "Let's go upstairs. Greta and Reagan can deal with the customers the rest of the night."

They made their way upstairs, and Alden shut the door behind them, locking it against the outside world. He swept Percy up into his arms, and carried his lover back to the bedroom where he tossed him onto the bed.

"Hey," Percy protested the treatment as he bounced.

"Get undressed. I think I want you to fuck me," Alden announced as he struggled out of his own clothes.

Percy's expression perked up, and Alden smiled, watching Percy strip and toss his clothes all around the room. Alden was more careful, folding his clothes and setting them on the chair in the corner. He didn't normally take so much time, but he wanted to frustrate Percy just a little bit.

Alden wandered over to the nightstand, pulled open the drawer, and removed the bottle of lube. He tossed it at Percy, who caught it with an annoyed grunt.

"Can you possibly move any slower?"

"Is that a dare?" Alden stopped in the middle of the floor. "Because I'm pretty sure I probably could go slower."

Percy growled, shooting off the mattress to grab Alden's hand and drag him back to the bed. Alden laughed the whole time, loving the fact Percy was taking charge. He fell onto the blankets when Percy shoved him in the chest. He wiggled into a more comfortable position on his back with his legs spread wide.

He pumped his own hard-on, squeezing some pre-cum out to ease the friction slightly. Percy settled between his thighs, and trailed a line of lube from Alden's balls to his hole, before rubbing his fingers over the puckered opening. Alden moaned, lifting his hips to give Percy more access.

More lube slid over his skin, and he bit his lip, trying to relax when Percy pressed the tip of his finger into

Alden's hole. Alden braced his feet on the bed and pushed, wanting more of Percy inside him. Hell, if he could, he'd have Percy fuck him without stretching him, but Percy wasn't going to do anything that might hurt Alden. They were always careful about preparing each other first, no matter how much they wanted to fuck.

Percy then eased three fingers into Alden's passage, stretching and relaxing the muscles there. Alden's cock ached with the need to come, but he created a ring with his fingers and wrapped them around the base of his shaft. He didn't want to come until Percy was buried deep inside.

"Percy, please. I can't take much more," he begged.

"All you ever have to do is ask, love," Percy promised while slicking lube over his length.

Alden stared up into Percy's face when his lover leaned over him, positioning his cock in the perfect place to thrust into Alden. The first stroke in burned slightly, but Alden wouldn't let Percy stop until he bottomed out and they were linked in the most carnal way possible. Percy froze above him, and their gazes met.

Love burned in Percy's eyes, and Alden knew the same showed in his as well. There would never be anyone other than Percy for Alden, and even if Percy changed his mind after the first flush of excitement wore off, or when Percy's magic came back for good, Alden would let him go. He'd keep all these memories stored in his head for those lonely nights without Percy in his bed.

"Stop it. I'm not leaving you." Percy rocked his hips and nailed Alden's gland.

"Oh, wow! Do it again."

Electricity raced up and down Alden's spine each time Percy pumped in and out of him. He tried to keep up the same rhythm with his own hand, but, at times, he lost himself in the sensations of being totally claimed by the man he loved.

His climax sneaked up on him, and exploded through his body, spilling his cum all over his hand and his stomach. Alden cried out, his inner channel clamping down on Percy's cock, massaging the thick length to encourage Percy to join him.

"Shit! Alden, I love you," Percy shouted, as he flooded Alden with hot seed.

They trembled and shuddered together, drawing out their climaxes until their bodies couldn't take it anymore. Percy collapsed on top of Alden, smearing Alden's cum all over their stomachs. Alden encircled Percy's waist, keeping his lover where he was. He liked it when Percy used him as a pillow.

His heartbeat slowed down to eventually match the beat of Percy's, and he smiled at the thought of their hearts beating in time together. After a few minutes, Percy rolled to the side and they groaned as his softened cock slid from Alden.

Alden lay there a few more minutes until he was sure his muscles would listen to him. After standing, he shuffled to the bathroom where he cleaned up and grabbed a cloth for Percy. He washed Percy off, tossing the cloth towards the laundry basket when he was done.

Percy tugged the blankets down, and they climbed under them, snuggling close. He ran his hand up and down Percy's back, glad to feel there were no more vertebrae sticking out, like when Percy had first come back. His lover had gained weight steadily, and was almost back to a healthy size.

He pressed a kiss to Percy's sweaty temple. "I love you, Percy Harlow."

Percy reached out and patted Alden's hip. "I love you too, Alden Sparks."

With those declarations, they drifted asleep.

Alden wasn't sure how long he'd been asleep before the violent motion of the bed woke him. He shot upright and glanced around, trying to figure out what the hell was going on. His still-blurry vision spotted Percy bouncing at the foot of the bed.

"What the hell time is it?" Alden snarled as he scrubbed his hands over his face, fighting to wake up enough to understand what was happening.

"I have no idea. It's back, Alden! My magic is back and fully charged."

Percy jumped to his feet, and whirled around the room, joy in every line of his body. Alden blinked a couple of times and tried to focus on what Percy had said, but Percy's naked form kept distracting him.

"Percy, come here and sit with me. I can't think while you're dancing around completely nude." He held out his hand.

His lover took his hand, and laughed when Alden jerked him into his embrace. Percy hugged him so tightly that Alden thought he might have broken a rib or two.

"Tell me again what happened," he demanded.

"I had a nightmare, and it woke me up. The therapist told me, when that happened, to go and meditate. I should be able to work through the fear and anger while in a trance."

Percy started bouncing again, but Alden tightened his hold on him.

"That's good. I'm glad she gave you a way to cope with the dreams," Alden muttered.

"Anyway, while I meditated, I gathered my magic like always. Only this time, it was there the second I called for it, and I could control it like before. My power's back. Do you know what that means?"

Alden kissed Percy hard. "You're healed."

"Well, physically I'm healed. I still have a lot to do to heal my mental wounds, but I'm getting there. I can start working again. I'm going to go and see the Gypsy Councilman, and let him know I'll be accepting jobs."

"I'm so happy for you, honey. I know how frustrated you've been with not being able to contribute to the bills and stuff."

He flopped on to his back, taking Percy with him. Percy laughed, and they wrestled, trying to get the upper hand. Alden could have taken it at any time, but he wanted Percy to feel like he'd put up a good fight for it.

Finally, Alden pinned Percy to the bed with his hands on Percy's arms, and his knees on either side of Percy's hips. Percy panted, but his cock stood proudly from his groin, painting lines of pre-cum on Alden's stomach.

With a wink, Alden shifted and wiggled until his ass was directly over Percy's dick. He was still loose from their last bout of lovemaking. He let go of one of Percy's arms to reach behind him and hold Percy's cock steady while Alden impaled himself on it.

Percy's eyes rolled back in his head as his length was surrounded by Alden's heat. They both stopped breathing for a moment, when Alden had taken all of Percy inside.

"Best way to celebrate," Percy murmured, once he started breathing again.

Alden chuckled. "I thought so. I want to feel you in the morning."

He slipped his hands under Percy's shoulders and rolled, somehow managing to reverse their position without Percy slipping out of him. Percy took a hold of Alden's legs, draping them over his arms to give him a better angle to ream Alden's ass.

"That's the way," Alden encouraged while Percy began thrusting in hard and fast.

The scent of sex and sweat filled the air, along with their grunts and the slap of skin on skin. This time their lovemaking was rough and animalistic, like Percy needed to work out his excitement by taking Alden as hard as possible.

"Fuck!" Alden shouted as he came for the second time that night. Cum coated his front, and he let his arms drop to the bed beside him, not sure he'd be able to lift them anyway.

Percy slammed away a few more times before he stilled over Alden, and spilled his own seed into Alden yet again. Alden didn't mind, and, in fact, had the thought he'd probably quite happily bottom for the rest of his life, if Percy was the one fucking him.

"Damn it, Alden!" Percy cried out as he climaxed.

After they could move, they repeated their actions from earlier, and ended up cuddling under the blankets again.

"I think you might have worn me out completely this time," Percy confessed. "I don't think I'll be dreaming at all now."

"Good. Go to sleep, and worry about tomorrow in the morning."

They went to sleep again, entwined in each other's arms, which was the most perfect place in the world for both of them.

Chapter Thirteen

Percy stood in front of the Gypsy Councilman's office door, and tugged on his sleeves. God, he hated coming to the High Council building and talking to the man, but it was the only way Percy could let him know he was ready to accept new jobs.

"Mr Harlow, the Councilman will see you now," the secretary said after he'd hung up the phone.

"Thank you."

He went in, and sat where the Councilman pointed. Percy leant back in his chair, and crossed his legs. He wouldn't fidget or show any nerves. The Councilman liked to play games to see how frustrated he could make a person meeting with him. Percy had gone through a few meetings, and wasn't going to be drawn in to entertain the Gypsy.

"Percy Harlow, how are you?"

The Gypsy Councilman was an older Gypsy, with wrinkled skin and silver streaking his gold hair. Percy had often tried to guess the man's age, but had never seemed to get it right. No one really knew how old the Gypsy was.

"I'm fine, Councilman Lobe. Actually, I've come to formally announce I have my magic back, and will be accepting jobs, starting today." Percy kept his face expressionless, not wanting Lobe to know how excited the knowledge made him.

"That is good news, Mr Harlow. I'm glad to hear you are no longer blocked. May I ask what method worked for you?"

Something about the sparkle in Lobe's faded lavender eyes told Percy that the Councilman knew exactly what method had healed Percy.

"It's rather personal, sir."

Lobe nodded. "Understood. I'll mark you as available on all the Gypsy manifests for when people come looking for jobs."

"Thank you." Percy started to stand, but Lobe held up a trembling hand.

"I wanted to talk to you about something, Percy."

Percy jerked, startled that the Councilman had called him by his first name. It wasn't the usual protocol for such a meeting.

"All right, sir."

"As you can see, I'm getting older, and I need to start looking for my successor." Lobe chuckled. "And, while your father believes it should be him, I have a different idea."

"Are you saying what I think you're saying?" Percy felt his mouth drop open. His first inclination was to say no. He'd never been ambitious enough to be a Councilman. It had always been his father's dream.

"No, it's not what you're thinking, young man. I don't want you to take my place. I know you have no interest in politics—or anything like that. Not that I can blame you. It's a soul-draining job." Lobe shook his head. "I don't know why anyone would want it."

"Then, if you aren't going to name me as your successor, what do you need to ask me?" Percy relaxed back into the cushions of his chair.

"While you wouldn't make a good Councilman, you do have a good head on your shoulders. Somehow, despite your father's interference, you've managed to surround yourself with quality friends, and not just Gypsy friends." Lobe shuffled some files in front of him. "I'd like you to look at the four Gypsies I've chosen, and tell me what you think of them."

"But I don't spend much time in Gypsy society, sir," Percy reminded Lobe.

"I know, and that's why I want you to help me. Use your connections to tell me which one might be a good choice."

"Are you sure I'm the right person for this job, sir? Maybe you should ask my father or my sister to help you."

Lobe shook his head. "No. Your father is one of the four, and, while Kiki is a delight, she's very flighty. I need someone I can trust to do this for me. I trust you, Percy."

After standing, Percy accepted the files from Lobe. "I'll do my best, sir."

"That's all I expect you to do. There may be more jobs for you when you're done with that."

Percy left Lobe's office, and took a sled back to his apartment. None of it made any sense, but he would do as Lobe asked, and hopefully not end up destroying someone's career, or life, in the process.

He went into the pub, and called for Alden. His lover came out from the back office, smiling when he caught sight of Percy.

"You're back sooner than I thought you'd be. Must have gone well with the Councilman."

Alden kissed him, and Percy let the folders drop to the floor as he pulled Alden closer. Why couldn't he get enough of this man? What kind of connection existed between them that made it impossible for him to go more than an hour without wanting Alden in every way possible?

Greta's wolf whistle broke them apart, and Alden sent a rude gesture in her direction. Laughing, Percy crouched to pick up the folders. Alden helped him, and Percy took a seat at the bar, hanging out while Alden and Greta got it ready for the customers.

"Councilman Lobe wants me to look at the four candidates he's chosen. He's planning on naming his successor soon, and wants to make sure he picks the right one."

Alden stopped polishing a glass to stare at Percy. "Why did he pick you to do it?"

Percy shrugged. "He says I'm honest and he trusts me. My father's on the list."

"Maybe he knows you won't nominate your father if you think one of the others is better. You're not 'family' above all else." Alden tapped the folders with his finger. "Are these the candidates?"

"Yes. Lobe also told me to use my connections to do some research on the four."

"It's a good idea. Chal will help, and maybe Steril would like to help as well, though I'm not sure if we'll be seeing him for a while. He was pretty shook up after he found out about Jackie."

Alden finished drying the glasses, and setting them up along the back shelf of the bar area. Percy loved to watch Alden work. There was such grace and confidence in his lover's actions, much like how Alden made love. Percy shifted on the stool, grimacing as his erection pressed against the buttons at the front of his pants.

"You wouldn't be in that predicament if you didn't think such dirty thoughts," Alden teased, as he passed to go into the back room for a keg of ale.

"Maybe if you weren't so gorgeous and such a good lover, I wouldn't be thinking about having sex with you." Percy teased right back.

Greta choked on her laughter as Alden had to stop and adjust the bulge in his pants as well.

"Thanks for that. We aren't remotely close to being ready to open, and now I have to set up with a hard-on," Alden complained.

"I'm going upstairs to go over these files. I'll come back down in a little bit to help out if you need me." He leaned over the bar to kiss Alden.

"That would great. One of my waitresses called in sick, and I don't want to be down one tonight." Alden shuddered.

"Oh, that's right. It's the big rival game between the Golds and Greens."

Greta wiped off the top of the bar. "Yeah, so everyone and their brother will be here to watch the game."

Percy winced. "Maybe I should stay upstairs tonight. I'm not sure I want to risk working."

When the Golds and Greens played, the crowds tended to get rowdy and loud. Alden's security did a good job keeping everything under control, but fights still broke out from time to time.

"I'll drag your ass down here, so don't think about reneging on your offer," Alden threatened.

"Fine." Percy headed towards the outside staircase leading up to their apartment. "I'll be back down in about an hour or so."

"Love you."

He waved his hand back at Alden before climbing the stairs and Percy unlocked the door to slip inside. He tossed his keys and phone on the table in the kitchen before grabbing a bottle of ale out of the refrigerator.

After opening the bottle, he scooped up the folders and went into the living room. He curled up in one of the chairs, set his ale on the end table, and flipped open the first folder. There was a picture of an older Gypsy, and Percy realised he'd seen the man around Alden's pub from time to time. Never caused problems, and was nice to the wait staff. He'd get Chal and Steril to do some digging on him, but Percy had a feeling the guy would turn out to be pretty clean.

The second folder was his father's, and Percy set it aside. He wouldn't recommend his father to take Councilman Lobe's place. His father was far more interested in advancing his own wealth and social status, rather than helping his fellow Gypsies. Percy didn't doubt that his father would be susceptible to bribes and other payoffs.

Something about the Gypsy in the third folder caught Percy's gaze. As he studied the man's face, he noticed how cold the man's eyes were and every instinct in Percy screamed that the Gypsy was dangerous and not someone to trifle with. Yet that didn't immediately take him off Percy's list. A dangerous man was a man who got respect, and any Councilman needed to be respected.

After standing up, he went to the desk on the other side of the room. He picked up his tablet, and went back to the chair. He opened it, and started four documents, writing down his thoughts from just looking at the pictures of the Gypsies. He'd fill in more as he read their files.

Percy made sure it was all noted before he grabbed the last folder and opened it. He held up the picture and studied it. There was something familiar about the Gypsy in the photo, but Percy was pretty sure he'd never met the man before in his life. It didn't mean he hadn't been in the pub at some point, and Percy remembered getting a glimpse of him in passing.

He set the picture on the coffee table in front of him while he jotted down his thoughts on the fourth candidate. After that, he read all the papers in each file, cringing only slightly when he read his father's papers.

More notes were added to each document, but, whenever Percy had a free moment, his eyes drifted to the fourth Gypsy. What was it about the picture that caught Percy's attention? Percy didn't attend most of the Gypsy social balls and meetings, so he wouldn't have run into the man there.

Everything he'd read said the man was a model citizen. Never got in trouble for anything. Had been married for a long time to the same woman, which was an amazing feat in the Gypsy society.

His phone rang, and Percy shut all the files and his tablet. He answered without checking the ID.

"I'm on my way down, Alden. Sorry I got caught up in those files."

"I heard Lobe gave you the files of the four candidates he's looking at to replace him."

Constantine's voice shot over the phone, and Percy grimaced. Thank God, he hadn't turned on the video screen.

"I'm not going to say one way or the other, Father. It's none of your business." Percy dashed into the bedroom, and changed clothes as quickly as he could while on the phone.

"It is my business. I know I'm one of the four, and you're my son. Of course, you'll be recommending me as the next Gypsy Councilman." Constantine sounded confident about that.

"I will be? How do you know that?" Percy paused long enough to shove his feet into some shoes before he grabbed his keys and shot out of the apartment.

Constantine exhaled loudly into Percy's ear. "We're family, Percy. Family takes care of each other."

"Oh, really? Were you taking care of me when you told Lobe not to give me any jobs because I was on drugs? Were you taking care of me when you locked me up in my room the first time I wanted to leave?" Percy stopped outside the side door of the pub.

"It was for your own good, Percy. You weren't ready to live on your own. Also, I was sure you were on drugs, or else why would you want to leave the compound and try to make it on your own?"

Percy snorted. "Stow it, Father. I'm not going to talk to you about this. Whatever my decision is, it'll be because I believe the man I recommend is right for the position. Not because he's my father. I have to go."

He hung up and turned his phone off. If he didn't, his father would be calling him all night, and Percy didn't want to deal with him. He went into the pub, and the wave of noise almost bowled him over.

After grabbing an apron and order book, he checked in with the other wait staff to find out who had which tables. Once that was taken care of, he plunged into working, taking drinks orders, and delivering them to his customers. Alden winked at him when he picked up the drinks.

"Excuse me, young man. May I ask you a question?"

Percy swung towards the voice, and almost dropped his tray. The Gypsy from the fourth picture stared back at him, probably just as surprised by Percy's reaction.

"Certainly, sir. How may I help you?"

As long as the man didn't ask him about recommending him to Lobe, Percy figured he could help the man out.

"Is the man who owns this pub here tonight?"

Percy frowned. "Alden? Yes, he's behind the bar."

A look of happiness and fear shot across the Gypsy's face. "Good. Thank you."

"Do you want me to give him a message from you?" Percy wanted to know the man's name. For some reason, there hadn't been a name attached to the Gypsy's folder.

"No. That's all right. If I want to talk to him, I'll go up there myself." The man turned to look towards the bar.

"Fine. If you need anything else, just flag me down. This is my section."

Alden's pub was old-fashioned in the fact that the wait staff were real people, instead of using video screens and electronics to get the customers' drinks. Alden liked the personal touch, and Percy had to admit that it certainly made for a friendlier environment, even if it did make him feel like he'd worn his feet to nubs by the time his break came around.

"How are you doing, love?" Alden set a glass of Pillian wine down in front of Percy when he dropped to the stool at the end of the bar.

"You owe me a foot massage," he told Alden, before taking a sip.

"Of course. I appreciate you helping out." Alden went over to fill some orders before returning to stand by Percy. "Are you having a good night, though? No trouble with anyone?"

"No. Oh, some Gypsy asked about you, and the weird thing is he's one of the four I'm looking over." Percy rested his chin on his hand and stared at Alden.

Alden shrugged. "It is weird, because most Gypsies would usually come up and talk to me. Did he give you a message or anything?"

Percy tapped the fingers of his other hand on the counter. "No, he didn't. Said if he ended up wanting to talk to you, he'd come up to the bar. He had the oddest look of excitement and fear on his face when I told him you ran this place."

"Nothing we can do about it until he makes a move." Alden nodded at Greta. "I have to get back to working. You have another five minutes before you have to get back out on the floor."

"I know. I'll finish my wine and jump back into the fray in a minute."

Percy did just as he'd said he would. By the end of the night, he was exhausted, but he'd made a healthy amount in tips, though he told Alden to give his to the sick waitress. Percy didn't need the money, not when he made three times as much doing jobs for people.

They locked the doors, and cleaned up before heading upstairs. Percy went right to the bathroom to start the tub filling with water. He wanted to sit and soak in a hot bath until all his sore muscles relaxed enough for him to sleep.

"You take a bath. I'm going to grab something to eat, and head to bed."

"Why aren't you sore?" Percy asked, as Alden patted his butt before heading out to the kitchen.

"Because I'm used to spending hours on my feet, and you aren't," Alden called back to him.

"True," Percy muttered, and sighed as he sank into the steaming water. He folded a towel to rest his head on, and leant back, closing his eyes.

He floated for minutes, or maybe hours, before the water got so cold he started to shiver. Percy climbed out of the tub, let the water out, and dried off. He didn't bother getting dressed since he was going to head straight to bed. When he looked into the bedroom, he noticed their bed was empty.

As he entered the living room, he spotted Alden sitting on the couch staring at one of the photos. When he got closer, Percy realised it was the picture of the fourth Gypsy, the one who was at the pub earlier that night.

"Who is he?" Alden's question was soft.

Percy joined him on the couch. "I don't know. For whatever reason there isn't a name to go with this one. I assume he has one, since we all do, but Lobe must have decided not to include it with the packet of information."

"How are you supposed to be gathering intel on these Gypsies if you don't have their names?" Alden frowned when he looked at Percy. "It doesn't make sense."

"I know." Percy rested his chin on Alden's shoulder, studying the picture in his lover's hand. "Do you know this man?"

"No, but there's something familiar about him, isn't there?"

Apparently, Alden felt the same thing Percy did.

"Yes, that's the exact thing I thought when I looked at his photo. It's like I know who he is, but can't place where I've seen him before."

Percy glanced at Alden, then back at the photo. He gasped as a thought hit him.

"No way. It can't be. The Gypsy trait is a dominant gene. If one parent is a Gypsy, then the child is a Gypsy as well," Percy muttered while snatching the picture out of Alden's hand.

"What are you babbling about?" Alden tried to yank his hand away when Percy grabbed him and dragged him off the couch.

"Come with me."

He led the way into the bathroom, placing Alden in front of the mirror. He held up the picture right next to Alden's face, so they could see both the reflections.

"Who does he look like, Alden? Ignore the colour of the eyes and hair. Just look at the shape of the face, jaw and nose. How his lips curve and the slash of his cheekbones."

Having Alden's reflection next to the image, Percy could see all the similarities, and nervous excitement started to flare in him.

"I think we've found a relative, Alden."

Alden shook his head. "It's not possible. Just like you said, when a Gypsy has a child, that child is a Gypsy."

"I'm not saying he's your dad, but he has to be related to you."

Alden met Percy's gaze in the mirror. "Do you really think so?"

Percy nodded. "I do believe it."

"If I have family out there, why haven't they come looking for me before this? I'm not sure I want to know any of my family, if they were willing to allow me to go to a workhouse instead of a good home."

Alden tossed the picture into the sink, and stalked from the bathroom. After collecting it, Percy returned it to its folder before going in search of Alden. He had to get dressed when he realised Alden might be down in the bar. Somehow, his lover had got downstairs and was pouring a drink by the time Percy found him.

"God, you must have sprinted down here." Percy huffed as he braced his hands on the bar.

"Would you like a drink?"

Alden held up a bottle of Angel liquor. It tasted like heaven while you drank, but you felt like hell the next day. Percy didn't want to suffer that in the morning, so he shook his head.

"Why do you think he's come looking for me now? I'm successful, and I have a great relationship with you, my best friend. I have great friends as well, and they're my family. I don't need anyone blood-related to me to have a family."

Alden ranted while drinking, and Percy let him. Finding out he really did have family, and they might be interested in meeting him after all these years, had to be a shock to Alden's system.

A knocking on the pub door caught Percy's attention. He wandered over to check who was out there, while trying to keep an eye on Alden. Peering out of the window, he sighed when he spotted the Gypsy from the photograph. Great timing, again.

"Alden, do you want to talk to the Gypsy who might be related to you?" Percy asked before he opened the door.

"Why?" Alden narrowed his eyes at Percy. "You didn't invite him here, did you?"

"I wouldn't do that, and you know it. No, he's outside right now. I assume he gathered his courage to come and speak to you." Percy didn't wait for Alden's reply. He unlocked the door, and waved the Gypsy inside. "Be careful. He's been drinking, and he's not happy."

"How did you figure out who I was?" The Gypsy wrung his hands.

"We have your picture, and, you look so much like him, it's pretty obvious once you see it."

"My name is Alosh, and I'm Alden's uncle." Alosh approached the bar area cautiously.

Alden watched him walk closer with angry eyes. "Why did you wait until now to come and find me? Why now? What's changed?"

"What changed was my father died, and, with his death, I was released from his rule. I've known you existed since you were born, Alden. I just didn't know where Alicia had hidden you." Alosh eased onto one of the stools, not making any sudden moves, and seemingly not expecting Alden to welcome him with open arms.

"I don't understand."

Percy walked behind the bar, and pulled down another glass. "Would you like something to drink, Alosh?"

"Just water." Alosh pulled a picture from his pocket and pushed it across the bar towards Alden. "Alicia was my twin sister, yet, for some reason, she wasn't a Gypsy. It was like all the magic came to me, and there wasn't any left for her."

After giving Alosh his water, Percy peered over Alden's shoulder at the picture. It was of a young woman, maybe about eighteen. Alosh had his arm around her, and they looked happy. Even though she was plain, like ordinary Beasors, and Alosh was bright and golden like a Gypsy, Percy could still see the family resemblance.

"My mother was your twin sister?" Alden shoved his glass aside and studied the picture.

"Yes. You look exactly like her, which was how I figured it out when I saw you a couple of days ago at a coffee shop on the other side of Catalai. It took me a little while to find out where you were living. Then, when I showed up, I wasn't sure how you'd react to family just dropping in unannounced like that, especially if you thought you didn't have any." Alosh dropped his gaze to the glass of water he held. Sadness caused his expression to darken.

"My father hated Alicia. He was embarrassed by the fact that he didn't have two Gypsies in the family. Even when the doctors told him it happens with twins sometimes, he got this crazy notion that my mother had cheated on him, and that somehow Alicia wasn't his."

Percy snorted in disgust. "Did he really believe that?"

"I think he went out of his mind with rage at seeing Alicia didn't have any magic. Most sane people would accept the differences, and love their children anyway, but my father threw Alicia away. He sent her to live with a family who wasn't even related to us."

Alden ran his finger over the image of his mother. "Is she still alive?"

Alosh sighed. "No. The information I received told me she died shortly after giving you up. Unfortunately, with her gone, I had no real idea where to start looking for you, and my father wouldn't let me anyway. Like I said, he's dead now, and I have control over the family fortune. I was going to use all of it, if I had to, in order to find you."

"Why did she give me up?"

Percy encircled Alden's waist from behind, letting Alden know he was there for him. Alden leant back against him, relaxing into his strength.

"Alicia was living on the streets by then. The foster family my father found for her had kicked her out. They didn't like her any more than my father did. I think she got pregnant with you, and, once you were born, she realised she couldn't take care of you. She couldn't come back home because my father wouldn't allow it. I didn't have any way of taking you either."

Alosh wiped his eyes with his sleeve, and Percy believed the man. No one would get that emotional while lying. Percy squeezed Alden tighter, and Alden patted his hands before breaking away from him. Percy watched as Alden rounded the end of the bar, and went to Alosh, hugging him. It was tentative, but heartfelt. Tears welled in Percy's eyes at the sight of Alden finally being able to say he had family.

"Will you come back tomorrow, for dinner, and tell me about my mother?" Alden asked. "I'm going to need the rest of the night to process everything."

"I'd love to, if it's all right with your partner." Alosh gestured towards Percy.

"I'm more than thrilled to have you come over, Alosh. It'll be nice for Alden to get to know his family." Percy smiled at the older Gypsy.

"Thank you. I'll be back around six tomorrow night?"

Alden agreed and escorted Alosh out of the pub. Percy waited by the bar, holding the picture of Alden's mother in his hand. He winked at his lover as Alden approached him.

"How does it feel to join the ranks with the rest of us with family members?"

He squeaked as Alden swept him up in his arms and spun around. Percy wrapped his arms around Alden's shoulders, holding on. When Alden set Percy down, they had to stand still for a second, waiting for the world to stop spinning.

"I'm sure I'm not going to be happy with my grandfather, and probably with my uncle for a little while because of what happened to my mother." Alden shrugged. "But that's normal, right?"

"Sure it is."

They walked hand in hand upstairs. After shutting and locking the door, they stripped and climbed into bed. Percy allowed Alden to drag him close and they entwined their legs while they lay together.

"What are you going to do about your father? You said he was one of the four candidates, right?" Alden ran his hand over Percy's back.

"Yes, and I'm not going to recommend him. He isn't the right person at all for the position. He'd use it for his own gain, and I know that's not what Lobe is looking for in his successor."

"Do you already have one picked out?" Alden asked.

"Yes, but I'm going to see if Chal and Steril come up with anything that I should be aware of. From just reading the information in the folders, the guy I'm picking is the best one."

Alden eased back a few inches, so he could look down into Percy's eyes. "You aren't picking my uncle, are you?"

"Why would I do that, just because he's your uncle?" Percy shook his head. "No. I'm going with the third guy. He seemed a little scary in his picture, but he seems to have his head on straight."

"Good. I didn't want you to choose someone just because he was related to me." Alden sounded relieved.

Percy laughed. "Honey, if I wouldn't recommend my own father, what makes you think I'd recommend your uncle whom we just met?"

Alden shrugged, and they went back to snuggling. Percy rested his hand on Alden's chest in the same place he always did. He thought Alden had fallen asleep, but, when Alden spoke again, Percy realised his lover had simply been thinking.

"You do know that, no matter how many uncles, aunts, or cousins I end up with, you're my true family. Home for me is where you are, and if you're not here then it's not a place I want to live."

Percy pushed slightly, and Alden rolled over on his back. Percy leaned over to stare into his eyes.

"I never knew what family was until I met you. You opened your heart, your arms, and your home to me. I fell in love with you the moment you welcomed me and you became my family as well. No matter what either of us goes through, we'll always have each other."

In the dark Percy used to fear, they sealed their promises to each other, making their bonds to each other even stronger with each kiss and touch until they cried out, their pleasure spilling into each other. Once again, their lives and souls mingled together, creating a family of two with their own magical connections.

About the Author

There is beauty in every kind of love, so why not live a life without boundaries? Experiencing everything the world offers fascinates TA and writing about the things that make each of us unique is how TA shares those insights. TA lives in the Midwest with a wonderful partner of twelve years. When not writing, TA's watching movies, reading and living life to the fullest.

T.A. Chase loves to hear from readers. You can find her contact information, website details and author profile page at http://www.total-e-bound.com.

Total-E-Bound Publishing

www.total-e-bound.com

Take a look at our exciting range of literagasmic™
erotic romance titles and discover pure quality
at Total-E-Bound.